Middle Ag

Feel good in your forties

Christine Human is a writer who lives in Somerset
and enjoys walking her dogs in the countryside and
along the coast. She spends a lot of time in her
writing room.

Someone re-emerging unexpectedly from her schooldays causes Lynda to have a total rethink about the past, the present and the immediate future. Determined to avert a mid-life crisis Lynda takes control. She has a plan. After many years of being a housewife she finds a job. The here and now is more problematic. Everyone around her quite likes the way things are, Lynda is going to upset the balance. But the preceding years preoccupy her most. Can she re-invent the past? Can she become single-minded?

With limited time and excess baggage, her husband and mother in law, Lynda sets out to make this her best year yet. To be fair the past years don't offer much in the way of competition.

She makes a list.

Middle Age Spread

Feel good in your forties

Christine Human

Periton Press

© Christine Human

ACKNOWLEDGEMENTS

For my husband Doug, my best friend and sparring partner.

For Courtney who kindly captured the images for the cover and left the cream cakes for Ali, who can now do up her jeans again. The original picture of her posing for Middle Age Spread is now on the door of her fridge.

For my children and grandchildren who know better than disturb me when I've retreated to my summer house, unless they bring tea and cakes.

And lastly for the companionship and devotion of my dogs, Rosie the border collie and Suzy the cockerpoo who laze in the garden chairs, snoozing, until my laptop snaps shut.

At most she had half an hour. Lynda locked the external doors, leaving the keys in for added protection against unexpected callers. She wrenched the curtains shut blocking out the wintry February sun, past caring what the neighbours might think. She struck a match to light the first candle. Her heart pounding with anticipation — her lips dry, cheeks flushed. It took several valuable minutes to light the remainder but the transformation of a dull front room with faded wallpaper, the odd cobweb, and faded family portraits in Woolworths frames, to personal love nest was worth it. She chewed her lips. Need background music. With shaky hands she slid in the tape. God, we must be the only house in the street, probably the whole of Bristol without a CD player she considered momentarily. Leaning back against the wall, wide eyes darting everywhere she surveyed the room. Something was missing. A tantalising fragrance. That's what was needed. She lit joss sticks to mask the usual traces of furniture polish, chips and lavender water. The 1930's clock chimed the half hour; seven minutes gone already, prompting Lynda to dash to the kitchen. Opening the fridge, she saw the blue glossy, sexy, oh so sexy box, and carried it reverently back to the sofa. Tucking her legs under her, she nestled down, loosened her dressing gown, slipping it off her shoulders, exposing bare, heaving breasts. With the box balanced primly across her thighs, concealing her nakedness Lynda opened it, eyes wide, and lips pouting. The chocolate éclairs, filled to overflowing with double cream with a sprinkling of dusted cocoa powder across the deep sticky stripe of chocolate draped down the middle gleamed in the candlelight. And it was buy one get one free too she marvelled.

The first bite reminded her that sex should be like this, the second bite made her dream of multiple orgasms; the third gave her that slightly sick feeling as she remembered that eating two chocolate éclairs was no substitute for sex. Then Lynda remembered where she was, who she lived with, and why this year she was going to have to change not only her life but her past as well.

The letter inviting her to a school reunion, for a TV show, would expose her lifetime of non-events. It had stunned Lynda and as she sat ruminating, she formulated a plan of action. Ditch Dennis, the boring husband — annihilate Ivy, the mother in law from hell, and get a life. All these thoughts clattered past on a conveyor belt of dreams and nightmares intermingled with occasional lucid thoughts. Lynda looked down to see the empty box and a dribble of cream nestled in her cleavage. She retrieved it and sucked her finger thoughtfully.

ONE

Aries: the past does not have a look in now, and it seems like something exciting is on the cards – things may never seem the same again.

I can remember the day I was born as if it were yesterday, which is not surprising because it was yesterday, or last week if I'm strictly accurate. Well, I say born, but I mean re-birthed. I slipped into my allotted family, as you do, but conveniently fabricated my past intending to focus solely on my future. My job application had been successful and today was my first day. It was also my first day for everything else, being a working wife, juggling a family and being me, just me.

'Hi,' I had announced, entering the spacious office, 'I'm Lynda,' but as it was unoccupied no one answered. I'd arrived early – it being my first day, but my confidence was fast evaporating and the urge to creep into a corner with a chocolate éclair was becoming more desperate by the minute. At 8.58 I was

1

still on my own, reluctant to sit down or even take my coat off, whilst waiting for the office staff of Manley and Sons Traditional Sideboards Ltd to turn up. I opened yesterdays abandoned newspaper, went straight to the horoscopes and after reading Aries checked out Gemini. Either your relationship isn't what you thought it was, or your feelings are changing, so be prepared...... Oh dear, didn't look so good for Dennis did it?

I'd been ecstatic when the job offer letter had arrived, but if I'm honest, totally amazed. But when dreams become reality – well it's downright scary. I had a master plan, predicting for myself a satisfying future, also inventing a past whilst embracing the present – even Dennis, and his mother. I didn't know what I would have to give up to get what I wanted – maybe too much – but I wouldn't know until I tried – and I was going to try – so hard. Panting with the intensity of a Jack Russell burrowing for rabbits, I tried to concentrate on the breathing techniques I'd learned from daytime TV. If knees can be described as hysterical then mine certainly were! I had an almost uncontrollable urge to scream. Think éclairs I told myself, chocolate éclairs. My heaving chest fought to control my breathing and thankfully it was becoming more regular now, whilst my pulse ceased thumping relentlessly against my wrist and I hoped the looming tension headache would dissipate before rendering me totally incompetent. Concentrate Lynda I told myself sternly – think only of a long fluffy bun oozing with double cream, a perfect mouthful of complete satisfaction. I licked my lips then allowed my tongue to explore the inside of my mouth, appreciating the benefits of brushing for three minutes, followed by flossing and a mouthwash. Even that was a few minutes of sheer indulgence for normally I would have been chasing around after Dennis, (where's my white overalls?) and Ivy, (did I leave my dentures on top the telly Lynda?) his mother. But today I had been too busy flicking the newly acquired hair cut – short, but feminine and carefree accordingly to the hairdresser. It had taken me a moment or two to unwrap and slip into – well, struggle into – the ridiculously expensive tights that completed the outfit of standard black skirt and white silky blouse. Breakfast had been out of the ordinary too - Dennis had muttered good morning as usual before jumping three foot backwards, hitting his head on the eye level grill as he realised, he was talking to me, Lynda, his wife of twenty-four years, and not a glamorous intruder. He even forgot to ask if his sandwiches were ready. But of course, they were – plastic container, three cheese and pickle, it being Monday, sat on top of his freshly washed white overalls. His mates called him Whitewash though to be strictly accurate he was white gloss man, for that was his job with the housing association, painting, and decorating social housing.

The door opened and my colleagues –ooh that sounded nice, shuffled in – almost on time. I wondered if they'd notice my bulging eyes and startled expression, or could hear my throbbing heartbeat. I needn't have worried – they didn't seem to notice me at all.

'Hi, I'm Lynda,' there I'd said it – again. Their uncompromising stares said it all. I wasn't going to fit in at all. They were all young, confident and beautiful and I was middle aged blob, swimming in jelly, wallowing in self-pity. Should I just leave now? Then a bleached blonde, with noticeable dark roots, clearly the pack leader, responded.

'Hi,' she said, smiling broadly, exposing pink wired teeth and a large blob of gum, which she chewed enthusiastically. A girl with legs somehow reminiscent of the Eiffel Tower, who I guessed to be her second-in-command, obviously then felt free to participate.

'So, you're the replacement for Suzy Slut, are you?' I nodded, and just kept nodding. I had become an icon, a nodding plastic dog from the rear parcel shelf of a 1960's Cortina. Please God, I pleaded, help me. I've never asked you anything much before, well except for winning the lottery or finding me a millionaire to run away with. If you can hear me now, please stop me nodding, or breathing – I don't care. The gang were all staring at me now and I smiled apprehensively, a nervous giggle escaping every now and then.

An enormous cough from somewhere behind startled me and I became aware that suddenly I was the only one in the room left standing. The rest of the girls had magically sat down with hands poised over keyboards and I turned around to locate the owner of the cough thinking how like it was being back at school.

'Good morning, Mrs. Fisher, nice to see you, do sit down.' He got the benefit of my fixed grin and cracked soprano.

'Good Morning, Mr Manley.' I took the seat that he pointed out to me with a regal gesture rather unbecoming in a man and I slid onto the swivelling chair, assuming instructions would follow. However, as I had been a housewife for twenty odd years, I was rather doubtful that I would achieve anything that Mr. Manley may require that morning, or even this century. How the hell did I get this job? What on earth had made me apply? Fortunately, he then entrusted my care to the office manager, obviously well versed in staff induction, who offered me small achievable tasks throughout my first day.

I trudged home that evening - feet aching, droopy wrists and a throbbing headache. I was Looby Loo - the dithery, droopy indecisive girlfriend of Andy Pandy. I was wrecked, past it, a wrinkly. How could I work with all those young girls who had more experience of life than me and my husband and his mother put together!

The well-thumbed book -If you don't like your life, then change it – all but leapt into my arms when I glanced at it and as my new year's resolution had been to follow its advice, I tucked it under my arm and retired to the armchair with a soothing cup of tea. After a long hard day, it informed me, relax in a hot bath, with face pack and soothing slices of cucumber on tired eyes. I glanced briefly at the dust, hid the ironing under the cushions on the sofa, and, having carefully examined the books glossy photos, lit a dozen night lights whilst the bath filled up with hot, steamy, highly perfumed bubbles. I lay perfectly still and my tense shoulders relaxed, my neck loosened and my headache slithered down the overflow, along with my

5

insecurities, my fears of being mistaken for a grandma, and a sizeable chunk of my boring life. My thoughts wandered onto the letter that had arrived just before Christmas that had made me question my future and instigated the release of the opposition and hostility that had built up over the last twenty years, if not more.

I'm so pleased to have been able to find you after all these years it had started. And my memory bank promptly flooded and overflowed. Well, that's not difficult when you grow up in one street, marry at sixteen your childhood sweetheart, and move two doors down to live with his Mum who, apparently, hasn't long to live but still malingers today in our back bedroom. The boys had always had to share a room because Grandma lived in and, whilst she always insisted that she would not interfere, she always managed to cluck loudly at every opportunity and I reluctantly shared their upbringing. Dennis, a martyr to his hunched shoulders and absolutely his mother's son, had dealt with my newlywed trivial requests for more equality with tolerance but largely ignored them anyway so I had ceased moaning, given in gracefully and embraced their lives, their values, their dreams – which were unsurprisingly, realistic, dreary and painfully limited. I provided twenty-four-hour supervision of the house and contents, waitress duties, nursing responsibilities and a hundred and one other tedious tasks whilst sharing the lives of our two boys, Gary twenty-two and Mark twenty-one. I could hardly believe that they had grown into men and left home whilst the oh so deaf one had become a permanent fixture – my very own space invader. My thoughts returned to the epistle – every sentence of which was as clear as if was written on the tiled wall beside me.

The writer of the letter, Verity Osbourne-Box, who I had known at school as Verity Sanders confirmed that she had led a life of sex, debauchery and general good living, had been married three times, had a little London pad and a cute cottage in the country and was now working for the Channel Four on this jolly exciting (her words) new project. It was her brief to track down as many members of 3B as possible, as research for a documentary. All willing participants would be interviewed and their lives, which had started out basically the same, could be charted, examined, defined and generally pulled apart. As my grown-up years could be summarised on one sheet of double strength Andrex I was determined to make the next six months, before our big reunion in August the most glorious experience that would shake Verity Osbourne–droopy drawers-Box to the quick.

'Lynda, where the hell are you?' shouted dear Dennis.

'I'm in the bath' I bellowed, quickly concealing the cucumber under the bubbles and splashing water on the hardened white mask. His head appeared round the door; a look of utter astonishment appeared on his face.

'The-b-bath,' he stammered, 'You're in the b-b-b-bloody b-b-bath, and where's my tea then? he said looking around as if he expected to see a stray plate of egg and chips floating over the blue towelling dolphins adorning the floor. I too looked down, but I was merely inspecting the worn tiles.

'Oh look, there's the crack where Mark had dropped his submarine as a small boy.' Isn't it funny, I observed, how you live with all those things and don't notice them until you leave the house for a day? What else was I going to find that I had shared my life with, polished, cherished, or just simply ignored? Was my home falling down around me without me noticing? A hand appeared wafting cold air past my face, I blinked, oh dear, reality again. Dennis was talking, I stared vainly at his face, frowning, willing my mind to turn back to the present, 'Aah, b-back in the land of the living are you dear?' he glowered. 'You never have a b-bath at this time of day, are you ill?' My mouth finally nearly caught up with the conversation and I giggled 'Oh Dennis, do you know what they say at work when you don't hear what's said? They say you've gone into screen saver mode,' but Dennis's blank face stopped me short. Changing tactics, I informed him that omelettes were on the menu tonight adding that I couldn't cook them in advance, could I?

'No' he relented, lifting the seat and unzipping his flies. He looked over his shoulder, peering at my now speckled face seemingly determined to upset my tranquillity. Where had the romance gone, I thought pulling out the plug. I curled into the foetal position sighing deeply.

'See, it knackers you having a bath this time of day, my tea's late, and it smells like a brothel in here,' he concluded, pulling up his zip with a sharp tug. There he goes again - and how does he know what brothel smells like? Well he doesn't does he? As he banged the door shut the candles were extinguished and the last of the

8

water gurgled noisily down the plug hole, leaving two soggy green circles and me – a haggard, water logged, decrepit water rat.

'Bugger it,' I said rising, slipping into a faded quilted dressing gown. I headed for the kitchen and Dennis. He was sitting happily reading the sport pages as I cracked the eggs into the bowl.

'How was your day?' I asked, like I did every day.

'Same as usual, Dougie turned in late again, so the boss was in a bad mood all day, oh and,' he pointed a chubby finger at me, 'my sandwiches were a bit on the dry side, could you put more pickle in tomorrow?'

'Did you see our Gary?'

'Yes'

'Was he O.K?'

'I suppose so, didn't ask, should I have done?'

'He's fallen out with Nita again, have they made it up, please don't tell me he's coming back home?'

'He never said,' he shrugged, 'but they're always falling out, they don't know what marriage is about these young ones, first sign of trouble and they're off home to Mum, I've got no patience with them,' he declared. I put three plates on the table with fluffy cheese omelettes, side salad, and fresh crusty rolls.

'Shall I call Mother?' he said, as he did every night, before bellowing and banging a redundant broom handle on the ceiling. It always made me cringe, why didn't I say anything? I screamed inwardly but smiled and said 'It'll be nice, won't it, now I'm working, that I can pick up fresh food during the week.' He rustled the newspaper loudly before deigning to reply.

'Suppose so, but it'll be bound to be more expensive in the long run, and I don't know what Mother is going to think of omelettes for a main meal, she likes her potatoes you know, and come to that, so do I.' I smiled, an over the top indulgent smile, I hoped, and tucked in.

'I do hope that now you've been working two minutes you're not going to try and change my lifestyle overnight.' grumbled Dennis. My smile turned into a huge idiotic grin as I tried to imagine changing any of Dennis's habits, for in many ways he was old before his time and although I loved him dearly it was rather like living with an elderly, crotchety uncle.

'Evening Mother had a good day?' he shouted to the oh so deaf one.

'Oh so, so Dennis, it's very lonely here on my own now Lynda's working you know.'

Amazingly, although they had both acknowledged that I was indeed a working woman, god that sounded nice, neither felt the need to ask me questions, or even tease insignificant details about my job title, my colleagues, or even where I actually went this morning so, after tea, I cleared away, made the coffee and put my feet up in front the telly. As the theme tune for my favourite soap came on, my head dropped onto my chest and I slept soundly for the entire evening - well until Dennis woke me to enquire if I was making his sandwiches that night or would I have time in the morning? How thoughtful, bless him.

TWO

Gemini: Just doing what you're doing will get you nowhere now.

Dennis's predictions didn't look half as exciting as mine, but I was prepared to let him wallow in my shadow, once I had cast if off of course. My constant companion, that little black book, was filling up rapidly with all the things I needed to achieve in the next six months so I could face the rest of the class with my head held high. The list, which had started out neatly with clear objectives, had now deteriorated into a scrawl and most entries were accompanied by exclamation marks or question marks, or both and some were heavily underlined. Some I considered to be achievable and some just too scary to even consider.

'Cup of tea for you,' said Dennis with a smug grin, 'and I've brought you a chocolate digestive – your favourite.'

'The last time you made me tea England had just won the World Cup,' I said in amazement carefully shutting my notebook shut and securing it with the attached elastic band. Dennis reached out for it eagerly,

'I'll pop your book down s-s-so you can drink your tea' he said. Ignoring his outstretched hand, I popped it safely under my bottom and took the proffered cup and saucer, with the now melting biscuit glued against the side of the cup.

'What's it all about then – this little book?' he asked invoking his most nonchalant tone.

11

'Just scribbling Dennis, it's a long time since I've been at work, and I need to write things down, I'm worried I'll forget something.' The oh so deaf one then delighted in reminding me that I had never actually had a job, having married at sixteen and been a Mum a year later. I swallowed the bitter words that threatened to escape with my soggy biscuit. If she had seen the C.V. that Tina, my best and actually only friend, had dreamed up for me she would have known that I had wide experience in accounting, organisational abilities, possessed extensive managerial skills, and had vast experience in the day to day running of a small cottage industry though my home commitments had limited it to purely voluntary work It was true that I was industrious but the cottage bit was pure fabrication as we had always lived in this 1920's terraced house. Beyond refreshing the white gloss on the exterior at regular intervals and changing the colour of the front door with inset of heavy stained glass the house had changed very little over the years. Whilst our neighbours had knocked through their sculleries producing state of the art sixties style kitchens with breakfast bars and imaginatively built arches to create long thin lounges our house remained a tribute to the 1930's. I glanced up at the set of three flying ducks that had clung to the wall for ever and reflected on their sudden appearance on Antiques Road Show as a collectable. Ours unfortunately had suffered over the years. One with a broken beak as the nail holding it up had fallen out when someone slammed the door. The second one had a repaired wing damaged by one of the boys (I never did find out which one), when he flew his

Airfix model of Concorde indoors. And the third had actually been in half at one time (no one owned up to that either) and was re-glued. The brown stain from the join marred the appearance somewhat.

'Lynda, you're miles away again,' complained Dennis.

'Sorry, Dennis, did you say something?' I said licking each finger in turn anxious to make the most of my chocolate fix.

'Yes, you haven't asked me how I got on at work.'

'No, sorry - how did you get on, still painting the old folks' home?'

'We finished that a week ago – we're doing the day centre now, and they're having dusty grey emulsion walls with white gloss.'

'Oh' I replied, fleetingly remembering him telling me of the change of location. My hand slipped under my bottom and I retrieved a now warm book. There was something comforting in holding this dream book. And dreams can come true, I told myself.

'You got another letter today,' grumbled Ivy, 'that's the third this week.'

'Well, can I have it then?' I said stretching out my fingers with cherry blossom coloured nails, which was guaranteed to annoy her and I smirked as she tutted loudly.

'Bright red nails in my day were the sign of a loose woman,' she whined.

'Well, Mother - I do have some loose bits but they're firming up nicely with all this exercise,' I explained firmly. I was enjoying the brisk fifteen-minute walk to work which was just as well as I had never learnt to drive. Dennis had maintained that we were a one car family, and always would be, so what did we want two drivers for? A mere hint of a smile escaped as I glanced at Number 2 on my wish list; for my provisional licence was hidden in the lining of my work handbag and I had my first lesson with the Bristol School of Motoring booked - Thursday one p.m. The letter was finally produced from her cardigan pocket with a bundle of fluff and a cotton bud. I admired the thick creamy coloured, classy envelope and the stylish handwriting clearly done with a fountain pen. Cheltenham? No, didn't ring a bell yet, but then it wouldn't would it? I hadn't kept in touch with anyone who didn't live within spitting distance. As I extracted the sheets Dennis and Mother leaned forward expectantly as eager as me to know who the author was.

'It's from Sally,' I announced, skipping to the end, and then I read all seven pages which very briefly outlined her life after Manor Park. I remembered her as a quiet individual with round specs, chubby red cheeks and a dreadful sniff. However, as she was now an air hostess who had flown many long hauls with Richard Branson, I could only assume she had dramatically improved with age.

'Sally, Sally, Sally' repeated Dennis, clearly trying to place her. Dennis and I had even been in the same class sadly.

'Is she married?'

'No mention of a current husband, but seems to have a partner, part time by the look of it!'

'Family?'

'No Dennis, she chose a life instead' I snapped, suddenly, unexpectedly, feeling very sorry for myself. With a deep breath, and drooping shoulders depression hit me with the velocity of a roof tile snatched off a rafter by a 50-mph gale. Dennis assumed a goldfish expression shifting uneasily on one foot uncertain whether to answer me back and Mother shuffled sideways to the kitchenette, sniffing loudly.

'I'm just going to the allotment,' announced Dennis.

I opened my notebook. Number 12. Get passport — I underlined it viciously. Number 13. Think of somewhere to go abroad, with or without Dennis. Would he believe that I had a business trip that I had to go to? Where did people go on business trips and what did they do when they got there? To my utter relief the next day was again a working one. In my world I went to the office and then went home again. But I was enjoying every minute of it and was always the first one ready for the challenges the day might bring, of which there were many, when you had as little experience as me. But I seemed to be coping. My colleagues at work, or mates as they liked to be called, were great fun to be with, often arriving late, took long lunch breaks and had endless doctors or dentists appointments. The opening door squeaked giving everyone time to look busy and a badger like face appeared, smiling benevolently.

'Aah, Mrs Fisher,' boomed Mr Manly, 'can you come up to my office about eleven do you think?'

'Yes, of course,' I agreed, chewing my lip, wondering if I was in trouble. But he waved the Royal wave at his little girlies as he like to call them and the door shut with a hint of a creak. The girls were all young enough to be my daughters, the thought of which made me shudder and I was so pleased that I'd produced two boys. They were all confident, outspoken, and so positive in everything they did. They took to calling me Mum and squawking aloud, with flapping elbows, if I expressed any opinions that they considered old fashioned. It hadn't taken me long to get used to all their chatter although some of their gossip still took my breath away. They had told me that Malcolm in despatch was running a book on who he was going 'to have' in his fork lift. Well, my mind boggled and I always put a spurt on as I hurried past his cubby hole. I know I was years older than him, but if Cilla was to be believed he had ravished Miss Butterworth and she was all false teeth and twin-sets. Still, I'd been there nearly a month now with no sign of sexual harassment, not even a glimmer of one. I must say I was disappointed. The diet was working and I was already six pounds lighter. My skin was glowing and I thought about sex a great deal. Dennis thought about cricket.

THREE

Aries: There's lots of interaction between workmates. Mixing business with pleasure? Anything is possible this week.

Lolly, whispering reassuring little phrases like, 'Don't stand any nonsense, if he paws you — whack him,' showed me to the inner sanctum on the third floor. Following hard behind her I wondered if my bottom wiggled like hers and guessed that it probably did now, I had substituted comfortable court shoes for ankle breaking, toe squeezing, high heels. They were not comfy, totally against health and safety policies, and just so beautiful. As I slipped into them each morning, hanging onto a chair whilst I did it, I shed off the old Lynda and growled softly, alive again.

Mr Manley pointed to a huge battered leather sofa, covered the ear piece of the phone with his chubby little fingers, and whispered 'I'll be a couple of minutes Mrs. Fisher, trouble at customs in Düsseldorf, these exports are a pain in the neck.' I nodded, hopefully appearing knowledgeable, but idly wondered where Düsseldorf was. This was only the second time I had been in his office, the first being the day of my interview but then, absorbed in my jelly like can't do this trance, I hadn't noticed anything so I took the opportunity to look around. A large oval framed tortoise-shell photograph, I presumed of his wife, took pride of place on his desk and two smaller silver frames showed two smiling carbon copy mini Manley's, one boy and one girl. How I yearned for a desk like that. I decided to add it to my list. I want an office with a phone, a fax, a computer, and to munch on sandwiches, straight from the deli, wrapped in those noisy, almost impossible to open plastic packets, delivered by my secretary. As he was still struggling with his conversation — even throwing in the odd guttural comment I noticed, I gave Mr Manley the once over, mid-fifties, balding, with a considerable paunch. I crossed my legs and breathed in deeply immediately attracting his attention. His eyes slithered over me.

'Pardon?' he wailed down the phone 'Sorry, I missed that last comment, it's a bad line, can you repeat it?' I fantasised briefly about having an office affair with Mr. Manley in order to accelerate my rise to fame but then noticed his squat little legs swinging loosely from the director's chair and the illusion promptly vanished. Blushing deeply, I rubbed one hand down my thigh trying to persuade my skirt to lengthen and licked my lips hoping to introduce some moisture into my parched mouth. As I took a deep breath to regain my poise the top button on my silk v-necked blouse popped off and landed on the carpet. A frog eyed Mr. Manley shouted down the phone. 'I'll catch the morning flight, and sort it out myself, goodbye.' He hurried around his desk sinking to his knees in front of me scooping up the button and handed it to me.

'Mrs. Fisher,' he began, 'I know it's short notice but could you come to Germany with me tomorrow. My wife sometimes accompanies me, but she has her committees, the children and suchlike, and   flying

18

aggravates her prickly heat. I need a good woman beside me.'

'Oh, that's where Duffelcoat is!' I thought. He barely paused for breath before continuing.

'I suppose I should ask Miss Butterworth but I'm afraid her hearing aid is not all it could be and she talks about the War you know — her father was captured or something. I did explain, didn't I at your interview, that it may involve travel?' He hadn't at all, and as I had only been there a matter of weeks I was amazed to be picked out as what I assumed to be personal assistant status. I started to babble. 'Um, well, you see, I um.'

'Mrs Manley certainly wouldn't let one of those young things out there go with me, not that I would want them to you understand. They're all chewing gum and divided brain cells.' I was now slightly deflated – even he didn't fancy me apparently. So much for feeling young and attractive!

'Not that you're not attractive, of course, because you are - and sophisticated and elegant too.' I started to cheer up again and beamed at him. 'And mature, oh and married — so Mrs Manley wouldn't have a problem at all.'

'Um.' There, I said it again! The richness of the English language and I can only say um and I think that's slang. Mature he said — like a hunk of old Cheddar I thought.

'I'd look after you of course, stop all those foreign men chatting you up, buying you drinks, and trying to get into your, um.' Oh dear, he's saying um now.

'Your um.' I stared down; he was sitting like an obedient corgi at my feet. I inspected his sweaty

19

forehead, contemplated his twitching eye, and shrugged my shoulders dramatically.

'Oh, Mr Manley, I don't have a passport' I apologised. 'Yet' I added quickly. He leaned forward on his hands, stretching one leg behind him, attempting to get to a standing position again and Lolly bounced into the room. Her mouth fell open exposing a large globule of gum but as usual she was ready with a joke.

'So that's why you have shag pile carpet Mr Manley.'

'Mrs. Fisher lost her button, I was merely returning it,' Mr Manley huffed, but realised immediately that he had just provided Lolly with more ammunition.

'Go back to the typing pool, Lorraine; Mrs Fisher will be right behind you.' I jumped at the chance to escape with Lolly and we walked side by side along the long dark corridor. She lobbed a big beefy arm around me and whispered, 'You're in there girl, at your age you won't get any better offers, go for it' and she punched me playfully, knocking me sideways.

Over a meat paste sandwich at lunch time I opened my diary, and chewed my pencil pondering the wisdom of ticking as achieved, Number 20, having an affair. I didn't tick it, as not only had I not slept with him; we were not even on first name terms. But maybe another man, another day, who knows? I left it there for the future. But I guessed I would need that tick to pass the celebrity stake so I decided that I could maybe invent a lover. No guilt trip, no holding in my stomach, no worries. As I had no real desire to be unfaithful, I scribbled in a few details of my mythical lover, to make him more real. Must think of a name too and an occupation, and where we met, how we carried on. A hot flush seemed imminent so I snapped the book shut. Glancing at my watch, I decided I just had time to nip out and get Dennis that new shirt I'd seen in Asda last week. Although his hair was receding and his feet, I'm convinced, had belonged in an earlier life to a camel I still loved him but I was determined to improve his image — despite the oh so deaf one's insistence at kitting him out in hand knitted nut-brown baggy cardigans. I hurried down the precinct, grabbed a wire basket, and picked up the shirt. Then I saw the sign across the road in the trendy shop, which I had always avoided preferring M & S Designer Jeans Half Price. I longed for a pair but hesitated, for when would I wear them, and what with?

'Hiya' chuckled Lorraine as she spotted me, now Asda bag in hand loitering outside the Posh Shop. 'Getting a pair of jeans are you?'

'No, well yes, I don't know, maybe.'

'They're really cool,' said Lorraine 'You'd look great in them. Go on treat yourself.'

'Do you think I could?' I asked. 'But I wouldn't have a clue what to wear with them you see, would you help me?' She chewed her gum thoughtfully before sniffing loudly, 'Yeah, O.K.'

We were both late back and crept into the office vaulting over the dustbins and squeezing through the small kitchen window to gain access both blissfully unaware that, with our skirts tucked into our knickers our wiggling bottoms provided the first-floor polishing team with an unmissable spectacle. Lolly, who had missed her vocation as a tabloid journalist, had

21

recounted to us at tea break. She had been told by Malcolm in despatch, who was invariably looking out of the windows when there was work to be done, that he had summoned the workforce with an urgent whistle and three large sash windows were inlaid with baked bean faces, open mouthed and indeed dribbling when Lorraine had followed me in. I clearly wasn't the attraction as my knickers were worthy of a White House cover-up. Lorraine's knickers however, were reported to have come from Office World – advertised as a rubber band size 2 by all accounts.

I typed spasmodically that afternoon, unable to settle into a comfortable rhythm. My new outfit kept floating in front of my face but the real mind-boggling notions that accompanied it, all spelt out by a gum chewing Lorraine, had me spellbound. I should have known that I would have had to get a complete outfit and had been easily persuaded. My new trendy top was designed to be worn bra less – me at my age with no off-white supporting   bits to lift and separate! Lorraine said that I had the knockers so why shouldn't I show them off, 'I'm a mother' I had said lamely. 'You're a woman,' she had replied. I reinforced my doubts 'I'm a middle-aged married woman.'

She had snapped back poking my chest with her long talons, 'you have got a cracking figure and my brother Les fancies you like mad.'

'But he's only twenty-one,' I argued in a mysterious high-pitched squeak.

'Yes - and what he'd like is a bit of experience, if you know what I mean.' I dived out the way before she

22

nudged me in her normal elbow jerking, side splitting sort of a way.

'Oh,' I mumbled. 'But my sons are older than him.'

'Yes,' she grinned 'and how many times did they bring their friends home to tea just because they wanted a gawp at you eh?'

'Well, actually,' I replied 'Never, I don't think,' and I remembered miserably my gingham checked pinny and pink fluffy slippers and my — I shivered. 'No, never' I said firmly, not at all surprised that they hadn't come to see me. 'But,' I said resolutely, 'that was the old me.'

'Good on you,' screeched Lorraine, finally catching me a hefty clout causing me to send the outstanding orders tray straight down into the waste paper box.

'Hey, that's saved a load of work Lynda, clever girl,' said Lorraine, and I really think she would have left them there if I hadn't retrieved them. I sorted them out, stacking them neatly. I thought back to those happy ten minutes in the naughty knicker section. Lorraine had reached past me and pulled out what I could only describe as a bright red glimmering string affair and tossed it at me carelessly.

'Here,' she said, 'to go under the jeans - you don't want a knicker line showing, do you?' Like a giggling schoolgirl I handed them to the assistant who placed them in my bag with thumb and finger explaining that she wished they would sell them in packs of five as there was nowhere big enough to put the barcode so they didn't scan and it ruined her nails typing in the numbers. Suddenly everyone was pushing past me and I looked up from my dream world   aware that five o'clock had come around again and it was back to the good old life. I gathered my things together and trotted off home swinging my shiny silver carrier bag.

Dennis was amazed by the catwalk show that evening, but clearly embarrassed, muttered loudly about the cost and absolutely lost for words when I stripped off the sparkly top over my head leaving boobs bouncing.

'You'll catch your d-death,' were his first words followed swiftly by 'and what are the boys going to think?'

'They're not to know what I have or haven't got on underneath are they?' Staring directly at Dennis - I unzipped and dropped my tight jeans. The blood apparently rushed straight to his head and he turned a mulberry red colour. I was expecting it to have had an effect somewhat lower but enjoyed the long low moan reminiscent of next doors tom on heat.

'D-d-d- don't ever everever hang those on the line f-f-f-for my Mother, my Mother, to see,' he pleaded. I decided that his Mother had been very negligent not referring him to a speech therapist as a child for the problem was definitely getting worse. A little spasm raced down my back. When I had started my new life, I'd expected and had not been surprised to feel like a maiden aunt but today, wow, I felt like I was twenty-one again or probably in truth for the first time. 'God life is good,' I hooted, and landed Dennis a tackle good enough for the Welsh Rugby Team. I was instantly rewarded by hearing the subtle tones of the oh so deaf one banging on the wall with her walking stick. I hoped it made a dent.

FOUR

Capricorn: Others leave you feeling irritated, let matters drift.

Ivy always remarks that she was born on the shortest day of the year, but it is no surprise to me, for nearly everything about her is short, from her height to her temper. I wish that she would hibernate each winter and emerge with a smile on her face in mid-March or so looking forward to the new season, a new beginning. Blossom on the trees, birds nesting, longer evenings, the strengthening warmth of the sun. But Ivy was born to moan, and I've seen more ambitious goldfish — though her memory is clearly superior. But sadly, she remembers the bad things. She chews family arguments up and spits them out at regular intervals. And as she refuses to answer the phone on the basis that it is never for her Dennis has to reach over her to grab it when it rings.

'It's f-f-f-for you,' reported my apparently long-suffering husband — well it's a struggle isn't it, leaning over, picking up the phone and saying hello. I was pleased to see him wearing the new shirt, even though it was almost hidden under the cross-cable knitted cardigan.

'Hello,' I said cautiously, as he had not asked who the caller was, just muttered, quite loudly, about it being nearly teatime, and that his football was on in a minute and not to be too long as Mother was expecting a call about her pile cream. For years I had taken messages about cricket fixtures, bowls meetings and the medicinal requirements of Mother in Law from the local Health Centre and now it was for me so I turned my back on the assembled family –

'Lynda speaking.'

'It's Julie,' said Julie.

'Hello Julie' I replied, shrugging my shoulders.

'Do you remember me?' queried the caller.' No, but give me a minute, keep talking.'

'Do you want a clue?' giggled the voice.

'Yes.'

'I sat behind you and I used to put chewing gum in your hair.' She was going down in my estimation fast, but with Mother in Law glaring and Dennis tapping his fingers on the top of the television I was not going to stop talking now.

'Another clue?'

'Yes.'

'I ate your jam sandwiches and you cried.'

'You obviously weren't on my party list then,' I said playing for time.

'Definitely not,' she laughed, 'well, as we got older it got better, when we got into boys, and smoking and staying out late.'

'I didn't do any of those things,' I replied huffily.

'I know that's why we weren't friends but I always envied you because you had a steady boyfriend and beautiful blond hair and I was jealous as hell of you.' How little she knew; how much I didn't want her to find out the truth - so I concentrated on guessing her name and keeping the conversation steered on her past — not mine.

'I'm going to need another clue.'

'The Sound of Music,' she declared.

'Julie Andrews!' I screamed.

'I don't believe it, after all this time, how are you, what have you been doing, are you married, are you divorced? (I bet she is). If ever someone was born to lie down for England it was Julie Andrews, who was definitely no nun, had dubious morals, and whose idea of being good was directly related to her prowess in bed, and that was at sixteen, when I last saw her.

'Well,' she started 'I got married, mainly to get rid of the stupid name, but I married a total wanker so I dumped him sharpish. I had a great time for a couple of years but with a baby on the way I had to get married again. I'm called Julie Blackman now. We live in Birmingham, got two kids and I work evenings in a massage parlour, all respectable of course.' Now, before I started work, I would have found it hard to talk to Julie but with my eyes opened by the likes of Mandy and Cheryl I found myself saying that I couldn't wait to see her again at the reunion.

'Is that how you got my number?' I asked, and 'will you be coming along? We could meet up afterwards and you could see Dennis, again.' Dennis however had overheard the name, remembered her, probably from the bike shed like the rest of the spotty youths from 4B, and was now on his knees flapping his arms around like a swan on its maiden flight mouthing no, no-no-n-n-no. His face went from tile red to ash white and back again.

As the grill pan caught fire and the smoke alarm emitted an ear-splitting screech, I ended the conversation abruptly but promised to call her back

27

within a few days. Well if Dennis didn't want to see her I certainly did, I was ready for a good laugh. The meal, a little burnt around the edges, was eaten and as neither Dennis nor his Mother seemed inclined to talk, I had the benefit of reflecting on the past life of Julie Andrews. Instead of pudding that night we had the leftovers from the 75th birthday party of one of Mothers cronies.

'Pass the Marmite, Lynda,' ordered Mother in Law. I gritted my teeth — could she never say please? And Marmite on scones, it made me sick thinking about it. 'I can't stomach jam, it gives me wind she would say, and the pips get stuck in my plate.'

'Rubbish' I replied, thinking that crap would have been even more satisfying to spit out. And I wouldn't have said that two months ago either. I'm not sure that it was a positive move though as Mother glared and Dennis looked distinctly wounded.

'Julie Andrews, what a blast from the past,' I reminisced. Julie, now she brought an entirely new meaning to the word spread I thought as I smothered my scone with jam. My life consisted of spreading myself thinly, trying to please the world and my family in particular, to preserve my sanity whilst widening their horizons. Now Julie on the other hand associated the word with spread your legs, spread it about, and all other unsavoury aspects which were beyond my comprehension. Although I had no desire to be like her, I was sure that she would spice up proceedings and could encourage me to with my dream book, though she wouldn't know about it of course. It didn't seem fair that she could feed me titbits of her life whilst I had to keep everything under wraps hoping it all happened before the big night out. It just went to show what an empty life I had I suppose. I went out to feed the rabbit and wondered, sadly, for the very first time - why it was that a forty-three-year-old woman, me, had so much in common with a stupid black geriatric rabbit, except the one tooth and bald bottom. It just about summed up my world really, I thought, tossing it a lettuce leaf to suck.

FIVE

Aries: Spending time in a new place will bring release.

'You've two days holiday due,' explained Doreen in accounts. 'Can you take them next week? If not, you'll lose them anyway, it's the end of the year,' she added. How can a year end in March I wondered, but not for long as she continued in her usual whining nasally whimper. 'The financial year that is, not the Chinese year, which I believe is in February sometime. I think this year is the Year of the Rat.' By this time, I had of course switched off to Doreen and considered my own end of year which, it occurred to me, was actually never ending. My year was a loop tape, constantly playing the same old tune. Although I was now working in a proper job, I was unable to cast off my old existence which clung mournfully around me like a damp fog. Dennis breezed in on a regular basis — mealtimes, bath times, filling his bucket to wash his car. Mother in law, like a hailstorm, dropping dark cold spiteful hints, casting a dark mist over my so-called free time. She constantly reminded me that it was her intention that the housework wouldn't suffer, as she would, through thick and thin, piles and catarrh, keep the house going. Yes, it was the year of the rat — I could see that now. Why did she make it sound like an admonishment, that me working was as if I was letting the side down? And the boys, well men actually, they appeared like regular little downpours, clouds that appear effortlessly, silently from a previously uncluttered blue sky just after you've put out a line full of washing.

'How's it going, Mum? Could you do my washing and I'll pick it up tomorrow because we're going out on the beer again tonight.' Pause for breath before continuing, 'You haven't seen my football boots, have you?' I was aware suddenly of Doreen tapping her foot impatiently.

'Two days holiday – well that was unexpected as I've only just started — um will Thursday and Friday be OK?' I muttered. Inwardly my mind screeched and churned. Oh no, it'll be like the old days, getting up, making sandwiches, making beds, writing shopping lists and enduring long boring conversations with the oh so deaf one about the neighbours, or the local postman's bunions. I trotted back to my shared office and confided in my new found friends that being at work was infinitely preferable and I was going back to Doreen and tell her so.

'Wait a minute there,' interrupted Polly. 'There's got to be something better than that.'

'Yeah,' said Lorraine 'Stopping in bed for two days with that new flashy salesman, have you seen his arse?' A chorus of oohs and aahs assured me that they had and I wondered why it was that I never noticed things like that - was it because I was a lot older than them or had I just got out of the habit? No — sadly I realised I had never acquired that particular habit. I resolved to home in on his bum at the first available opportunity. However, this didn't solve my immediate problem — that of two free days. I sat that evening watching Mother knitting squares, Dennis cutting his toenails and re-read some of the letters from my old school friends. I tried hard to imagine their faces, nearly thirty years on. I glanced in the mirror and decided to have my hair cut again, and perhaps even highlighted. I scribbled it surreptitiously in my little book.

Sally's letter this month was all about the long-haul flights she was on with stopovers in Hong Kong, Florida and Brisbane. It's not as romantic as it sounds, she had complained, my feet throb continually until placed higher than my head, my complexion is similar to a Brillo pad and if that politician, who shall be nameless, but he's the one on Thoughts on Sunday pinches my bum once more I will expose him to The News of the World. Envy reared its ugly head. How could I meet up with her and explain my life, or lack of it? How long could I evade writing back to everyone?

'Dennis,' I said, 'Let's do something different for Easter, why don't we have a romantic weekend away, just the two of us?' I continued, trying not to stare at Mother, who bristled visibly, clicking her needles loudly. She could make a hedgehog crossing the road, caught in the headlights of a speeding vehicle, look relaxed.

'Don't you bother about me,' she snarled,'you just act as if |I wasn't here.' Dennis gulped and began his W-W-W and I interrupted with a 'Let me get you a cup of tea whilst you think about it,' escaping to the kitchen. Where did that come from, I asked myself, shaking with the absurdity of trying to change the family's habits of a lifetime. I returned to the vipers' nest with the tray - remembering the milk jug, the sugar bowl but had only loaded two cups and saucers, having forgotten Mothers favourite, the blue Denby, and Hawkeye spotted it immediately. She stood up bristling with resentment.

'I don't know what's got into you, since you've been working you've no time for me or my Dennis, you're rude, and I'm going to pack my bags and go and live in an old people's home. It's clear you don't want me here anymore.' And I had thought he was my Dennis! Dennis looked so dejected and my conscience hitting me on the back of the head was making me reel. I quickly fetched her cup and took it to the bedroom.

'I'm so sorry, I don't know what got into me, I'm just tired I suppose.'

'I usually have a biscuit as well,' she sniffed, 'but since you've been dieting, we've all had to suffer.' I marched back to the kitchen to collect a whole packet of custard creams, her favourite since her plate had been giving her trouble. I watched her dunk and slurp and wondered if she ever noticed the thick deposit lying in the bottom of her cup when she had drained the liquid. Dennis had meanwhile, turned on the football, grabbed a beer, and sat hunched up watching the flickering screen intently. Then the boys appeared, football scarves decorating their nutty brown cardigans.

'Hiya Gran,' they chorused to her empty chair. They slipped into their regular places, slid their shoes off, and cracked open their cans.

'I'm going to have a bath!' I informed the kitchen door. Why, having lived here twenty-five years, did I suddenly feel like a cuckoo in the nest? Ivy benefited by my outburst the following day too as I got up early, hung out the washing, took her tea and soggy toast in bed, and even managed a smile. Then I rushed to work, wondering if   roller skating would be an option to save time.

Lolly punched me playfully as I took my seat.

'Had a good think about your couple of days?'

'Yes, and I'm going to take them, I found an offer in the free paper for the health farm, Fradly Manor. A four-day special offer, all the treatments and lunch, including a facial and a hair do. I just have to work out what I can tell Dennis.'

'Brill' said Lorraine and Mandy agreed, but with a qualifying 'Yeah, when I get old, I'm going to do that too.' Mandy then came up with a suggestion that made me realise that this dream could come true.

'When I started here,' she thought carefully, before continuing 'I was crap, so they sent me to Coventry.'

'That's a shit thing to do!' said Lorraine. 'I'd have told them to stuff their job.'

'No, they sent me to Manley's Regional Office in Coventry you dimbo, I was put in a B & B and I learnt the ropes there, and the lads there, well they was brill. I went out with a different one each night.' They didn't need me anymore and I left them to discuss boxer shorts versus Y fronts, whilst I basked at my acquisition of the perfect excuse. I practised the wording, 'I have to go away Dennis, and they're sending me to Coventry, on a course.' By tonight I would be word perfect and by tomorrow I hoped I would be able to tell Dennis without turning bright red. Lunch break over, we all returned to our seats and tackled the mounting piles of paperwork. When the door opened, we all looked busy but it was only

34

Doreen. She dropped our payslips on the desk and I grabbed mine eagerly for my new lifestyle didn't come cheap, in fact I was spending every penny. Still Dennis had said that I should put it away for a rainy day and it had been pouring buckets since I'd come out into the big wide world. He thought I was tucking it away in a deposit account — whereas I knew I was placing big deposits on all my hopes and dreams. Guilt about excess personal indulgences hung heavy in my stomach though, ruining my appetite, no wonder I was losing weight.

Fradly Manor Health Club had the grandest gates I had ever seen, and the entrance stretched interminably in front of me. I bet I was the only person ever to arrive, dropped off mid bus stops by the friendly driver of a National Express coach, I thought, grasping my holdall tightly. The sign said Welcome, the information that the car park was a half mile up the gravelled drive was not so welcoming. I hoisted my bag over my shoulder and started walking.

This is a mistake, I thought. What am I doing here, what makes me think I can fit in with all these businesswomen, rich and successful? There was only one way to handle it then. Lie (again)! I considered my options; could I invent a marriage to a Doctor or a lawyer? My deceits, at first insignificant were assuming gigantic proportions the closer I got to the grand entrance. I considered talking in Pidgin English in the vain hope that I may be taken for a foreign Princess or, could I perhaps feign kinship with the latest in girl bands? I got quite excited about being someone else until I realised that I'd booked in as Lynda Fisher, giving my real address. It was no good – I pushed my shoulders back, took a deep breath, and licked my glossy lips. What seemed like a mile later I arrived, looked up at the wide stone staircase, admired the enormous open gothic double doors and looked nervously at the revolving doors in the marble floor entrance hall. I was   rather the worse for wear, having been splashed by passing four-wheel drives, all driven by thirty-year-old chicklets with large bank balances and designer boobs I thought despondently. Before going in I fished out and put on my fake Gucci sunglasses, took a deep breath and then practised my confident glide across the hall but the immaculately dressed receptionist soon had me quivering.

'Good afternoon,' she purred. 'Can I help you Madam?' That did it and the Dennis affliction hit me.

'I'm, I'm b b booked in, and I'm going to um, um.' She interrupted. 'Your name?' she smiled. How did she smile with her mouth whilst her nostrils flared with distain? Three ladies dressed in track suits and brand-new designer trainers hovered by the desk whilst I did the dance of the lonely goldfish-bubbling noise from my mouth, flicky fingers like impatient fins. Then the all revealing hot flush materialised when my name escaped me. It wasn't even on the tip of my tongue – at this point I was doubtful if I had ever known it. I could feel their interest grow; they grouped closer, gathered for the kill.

'I'll write it down,' I said, and the receptionist handed me a chubby gold fountain pen without blinking an eyelid, turning the register around. I was back in the first year of secondary school again covering my scrawl with my free hand to ensure complete privacy. Three pairs of eyes looked keenly at me trying now to guess my identity and I put my head down slightly to one side, half smiling, practising my regal stance. At this point the dark glasses were proving to be a liability but I felt around until I found the edge of the paper scribbling on the next empty line with quite a flourish. Their attention, fortunately, was distracted by seeing Jackie, yes, that Jackie, coming downstairs moving gracefully, head held high. It is her, I marvelled, it is her and I've been in the same room with her. Wow. Just wait till I go to work and tell them. I've read all your books; I wanted to scream at her. But of course – I didn't. She passed through, every step a star, heading for the treatment suite.

'She looks older than she does on the television, doesn't she?' commented track suit number one.

'She certainly looks much older than husband number three!' remarked number two, very unkindly I thought.

'Well, he is young enough to be her son, lucky cow,' sighed number three. 'Shall we join her in the pool then? We might hear some gossip?' They slid out of reception having forgotten me entirely.

'Your keys, Mrs Fisher, Room number thirty- nine on the third floor; I'll call someone to carry your luggage.'

'No thanks, I can manage,' I argued - there was no way some sneering lad was going to fondle my plastic holdall. I grasped the oversized golden key and following the signs, found my room. It was snug, but immediately relaxing, complete with a dish of fresh fruit, a vase of real daffodils, and big fluffy white towels. I could stay here forever I thought, and no paint covered fingers would ever tarnish these towels, as I sniffed them, hugging them close. I unpacked quickly and sat on the bed looking at the brochure. Book everything it stated, as soon as you arrive, to make the most of your stay. It was already 10 am so I phoned down to book a body massage, followed by a swim in their pool, followed by a sauna. After lunch, I would be taking another dip in the pool, then a leisurely frolic in their Jacuzzi before having a manicure, dinner and an early night. The bed was heavenly, all white, with gigantic square French embroidered pillows, and the sheet turned down at the corner to reveal a tasteful small bunch of lavender. I pushed the edge gently and my hand sank down straightway into a warm feathery expanse. What a waste to have all this on my own, I decided, but then quickly changed my mind as I considered the alternative. It just wasn't a Dennis place — he'd rather be in Butlins.

The pampering worked its magic and I was surprised to find that I could mix in with the other clients. I spoke carefully, and assumed a slight accent and when asked the inevitable question about my background I was evasive yet consistent with my replies.

'It's a company thing, a reward scheme if you like, and they'll get the benefits when I return next week on top form.' The ladies–who–lunch brigade looked suitably impressed by this and I only hoped they wouldn't see me leave. It was a long walk to the bus stop and hardly an option for an executive like me! The days passed in a haze of total pampering on a heavenly level and as I left after the longest break I had had since I'd been in Bristol Maternity Hospital twenty years ago, I looked up at my little room in the eaves and decided that next time I would have a private balcony. You're getting carried away girl — just hope that you can come back at all. I peered over to the car park, yes, it had been worth checking out early, and I hit the gravel drive. As I walked the birds sang and the misty sun warmed my back. My bag felt heavy though and I had to keep shifting it from the crook of one arm to the other. A squirrel skipped past and I followed its path until it skinned up a tree and disappeared. I wondered if I should stop and put my trainers on as the high heels were causing blisters already. The tree stump was ideal as a seat and I pulled the trainers out and debated changing into track suit bottoms too as the floaty skirt was not an ideal combination with blue trainers. But that would mean changing my top too and I didn't fancy being caught in my bra and knickers by a passing car. The trees were still wearing their winter coats and unreliable as cover and it was rather muddy to venture further in. I took the decision to put the track suit on top of my existing outfit and was just hopping around on one foot, one trainer on and one off as one had been catapulted into the undergrowth as I had flicked a towel out. Yes, I had inadvertently packed one of the embroidered Fradly Manor towels — only the pocket sized one. And then I heard a sound, it had to be a car, coming down the drive and I had nowhere to hide. Even I couldn't make a story as to why I had forgotten to pick up the company car! I had time to retrieve my trainer before I sat down and waited for its appearance, hoping that it would pass me by unnoticed, which of course it didn't.

'Hello, it's Gary's mum isn't it? I saw you yesterday in the conservatory pool when I delivered the bread. I always stop and have a little look through the windows, it cheers my day up. Once it was a nuddy weekend and I was there for ages. Right by the pool steps I was!! The spotty youth smiled when I nodded.

'You looked fantastic in that bikini, you did,' he added licking his lips salaciously. 'Do you want a lift, only two more drops and then I'm going back to the bakery, I could drop you at your front door if you don't mind a bit of a long ride, and I bet you don't do you?' Confident that I could floor him, if necessary, with a withering glance, I threw my bag onto the floor and climbed into the cab, glad to be anywhere except on the road.

'Thanks, um, Steve isn't it? But if you could just drop me off on the main road that'll be fine, I can catch the bus from there. The two-minute ride seemed like a lifetime as he chattered on about what he had done since leaving school – mainly delivering bread it seemed combined with a bit of clubbing. He still lived with his Mum, 'well its cheap innit and you gets your washing done and a meal on the table.'

'It only gets difficult,' he added 'when you wants to take a girl home, if you know what I mean,' he smiled broadly and I swear he was dribbling. He pulled into the nearest bus stop and whilst I was gathering up my bag, he shot round to the passenger side.

'Here I'll help you get down,' he grinned, opening the door. I slid down into his outstretched arms, to find his hands nestling my boobs, and with no shame at all he continued 'with my eyes closed, I could be kneading dough, warm, soft, but when I open my eyes, oh it's so much better.' I willed my nipples not to rise to the occasion, swallowed hard, and made my excuses.

'Nice meeting you again,' was all I could say as I realised that he was as unlikely as me to tell anyone of our brief meeting. I had been scared yet not terrified as I felt I could have clipped him round the ear and he would have stopped. My secret was safe I was sure and I could now add another experience to my dream book — sexual harassment. The bus ride back gave me a chance to catch my breath, adjust my clothing and slip back into my day clothes under the cover of what I thought was an empty top deck. I had forgotten however the drivers' covert camera, until we swerved madly and as I toppled forward grabbing the handrail, spotted the lens. As I had just checked my boobs by hoisting my top under my chin, pulling each cup of my bra away to check that my nipples had lost their pertness. I pretended not to hear the drivers throaty growl as I alighted 'and I'd wanted to be a window cleaner,' he'd laughed.

I reached home by lunchtime.

'Hi Lynda, we've missed you, had a good time, learnt a lot? Glad you're home, the laundry basket's overflowing, and we've run out of toilet rolls.'

'Hello Dennis, it's OK, I'm back now, - I'll just go and change.' The good feeling evaporated and my shoulders felt heavy again. Oh well, back to the real world.

SIX

Aries: This week you may ask yourself why you didn't look at the possible consequences before entering a certain situation.

I had tried to fix the blocked-up sink but failed miserably. Despite perching, legs wide apart, on the work top brandishing a long blue, Stone Age, sink plunger and pushing and pulling vigorously, even violently, the only dirty suds that escaped were the ones that now covered my clothes and hair. As globules of stinking, greasy water dripped down my nose I roared in frustration — just one more try. I summoned up every remaining vestige of strength and, holding the plunger firmly in both hands, crouched down and rhythmically tried to clear the stubborn blockage. The noises I must admit, sounded rather like vigorous lovemaking, not like mine you understand, but I had heard some once on a soundtrack from a video the boys had acquired but quickly hidden when I appeared. I suppose they thought I would have been shocked and, in all probability, they were right — at that time. But that was before I joined the real world. I pulled harder on my plunger and wondered what it would be like to experience sex that made you cry out loud. I then pondered what it must be like to be able to concentrate on sex whilst it was happening instead of using the time for making lists for re stocking the freezer, or even to think about who I might vote for at the next election. As I heaved again the mirror revealed my beetroot sweaty face, lank hair and clinging T-shirt. I gasped, groaned, grappling with the devils' tool, closed my eyes and pretended I was making love. A reassuring sucking noise was followed by giant watery explosions and I stopped suddenly, looked down, and saw the water level lower, but only slightly.

'Yes, yes,' I gushed. Dennis appeared at the window, proudly displaying his newly pulled rhubarb.

'What are you doing?' he enquired. 'Just having sex with a sink plunger dear' was my immediate response, though under my breath. I wanted to ask him if he ever had obscene thoughts whilst tugging at those long luscious pink vegetables, or are they fruits? Tucking them under his arm he wiped his runny nose with a muddy finger. No, I bet next doors tomcat had more exciting dreams than Dennis, and he certainly put more energy into it. I had watched him chasing Fluffy, what a hussy she was. And there's another of life's puzzles. How did Thomas know that he was a cat? Did he look in the mirror, or just overhear my conversations about neighbourhood moggies. Or did he exude a feline smell that enabled him to recognise a fellow cat? It's true I thought, that memories are made of smells and even though Dennis was beyond the aroma zone his odour remained locked in my memory banks, welly boots and damp compost. Polly said her boyfriend could smell if she had her period, and always had an excuse to not see her that week. Do I smell, with my hormone levels reaching critical, as if I am going off the boil? Dennis interrupted my thoughts, clearly waving the plunger had given him an idea of my objective, and he may also have remembered that I had been asking him for several days for his assistance.

'Have you cleared the sink then?'

'No, well sort of, partly, but I think it needs a real man to finish it.'

'You'd better find one then hadn't you.' Dennis chuckled. 'Just a little joke you know.'

'Yes, a very little one,' I replied, thrusting the plunger in his direction. His best efforts also failed, and his general apathy stirred me to open Yellow Pages. How did you choose a plumber anyway? By the size of his advert, by the sound of his name or by his trade qualifications. But I didn't know my NVQ from my Corgi so that wasn't going to help. Aah, that sounded promising. Trust a local with your U bend. Phone Dave on.... 'Yes, Dave sounds like a good name for a plumber, I'll try him. I punched in the numbers, waited to hear his voice. It wasn't too late to cancel him if he sounded dodgy. Isn't it great that those old dials on phones have gone for good; even Mum in Law had been parted from her Bakelite phone, tempted by pink plastic with memory re-dial? Those old phones splayed havoc with your nails. Plumbing and soft cuticles do not mix. I closely examined my nails - I wanted a pedicure, or was it a manicure? I could never remember, still as I probably wasn't going to get either this side of Christmas it hardly mattered did it?

'I'm sorry I can't take your call,' the gravelly voice announced. Promising I thought - he sounds like the man who reads the late-night news.

'Please leave your name and number and I'll get back to you.'

45

'Hi,' I said in my most sultry voice. 'Please call me back, I need unblocking, desperately.' I hung up remembering just too late that I hadn't left a phone number, or a name. Did I have the courage to ring again? Yes, well I couldn't go on like this could I? I went outside with the bowl of dishwater- narrowly avoiding smothering my roses with putrid greasy water. I jumped when the phone trilled.

'Hello,'

'Hi' said the voice 'I did a 1471 and you sound like the lady who left a message, am I right?' What's 1471 in the Karma Sutra? I wondered, turning red and gasping all at once.

'Yes,' I managed to croak, 'it was me, when can you come, I mean, when can you look at my plumbing?' Thankfully he interrupted me, took all the particulars, booking an appointment for the following morning.

'See you around ten then,' promised Dave, 'rod in hand.' Ten this evening would have been better, with a bottle of wine, candles and romantic music and rod in hand of course. What is the matter with me? I never used to think this way; before I know it, I'll be having erotic dreams about Tony Blair. I flapped my hands widely about my face trying to dissipate the hot flush. What am I thinking of? I don't even know what he looks like, he's probably fifty plus, closely related to my garden gnomes and flaunts a builder's bum. Still, let's wait and see. A shudder of anticipation tickled my backbone. I phoned the office, telling them I would be late.

Next morning, I cleared breakfast away - waved goodbye to Dennis, overalls tucked over his arm, and

Ivy, who was off to a coffee morning at the over sixties club. I watched his arrival from the upstairs window and was not at all disappointed by the broad-shouldered figure approaching. He sparkled like a Lego man, clean polished and chunky. I called him handsome — the girls would probably have called him fit. I dived downstairs opening the door as he was extending one finger to push the buzzer.

'Hello,' he grinned. Pulling the door wide I ushered him through to the kitchen, a Cheshire cat smile enveloping my face, so big it hurt. He slid past me carrying a large floppy bag which jingled merrily. Oh well, he definitely intended to do the job then I thought dejectedly. Once in the kitchen he poked gingerly through the grease laden overflowing sink.

'I can see you've been plunging so I'll start lower down if it's ok with you?' taking off his jacket exposing tendrils of dark curly hair peeking through his shirt. 'Let's open it right up shall we?' he asked with a wicked smile. I don't believe it; he's got a lovely set of teeth as well, and I'm sure they're for real. I attempted a closer look, but he had opened the doors to the cupboard and was already loosening the u bend.

'Have you got a bucket?' he asked as he lay flat on his back, head ensconced under the pipes. My, I thought, what big feet you have! And we all know what that means don't we girls we would have said in the office.

'I'll get you one,' I replied. 'Would you like a cuppa?'

'Never say no.' I'll bet you don't, I thought, popping the whistle on the kettle. I passed him the bucket, listened to his heaving and grunting whilst he freed the connection. The sink emptied and the bucket gushed almost to overflowing. Dave pulled out the bucket and then popped his head back underneath the sink.

'I think it was just the u bend,' his muffled voice explained. I reached for the teapot, removed the lid and disposed of the left-over contents down the sink. Dave howled, emerging dripping with dark liquid, tea leaves planted in his eyebrows.

'I didn't know anyone still used loose tea anymore!' he said 'But at least it wasn't hot.' I offered him a towel and a change of clothing, well it was the least I could do, wasn't it?

But the day didn't turn out as I had expected, and my quivers of excitement turned quickly to sniffs of disappointment as he pulled his shirt over his head, revealing his chest - which stirred long forgotten childhood memories of Bristol Zoo and Wendy the elephant's trunk. And then he coughed, following it with a raucous clearing of his throat, his chest wobbled like pink blancmange, and for one horrible moment I thought he was going to spit into my sink. I stepped back quickly fearing the worst.

'Hhhhhhh' said Dave, 'sorry, the cold makes me wheeze, but then, when you get to sixty you've got to expect a few little problems haven't you?' Sixty, sixty, my brain obstinately repeated.

'I ought to think about retiring, taking it easy, but I wouldn't know what to do all day, do you know what I mean?'

'What do I care?' was what I wanted to say, but I just nodded vaguely. Sixty, he's sixty, his words echoed around my head. Good god, I ought to be eyeing him up for the oh so deaf one - not imagining spit roasting him in my kitchen. I'd thought I'd been admiring a proud turkey but when the feathers were off, I'd been confronted by a scraggy old chicken. Worryingly, if he hadn't taken his shirt off, I'd never have guessed. There ought to be a law prohibiting the impersonation of younger men. Even Cliff Richard had let his neck wrinkle gracefully. And to think that I had considered enjoying wild passionate sex on the lino with him. I held my hand to my mouth and gulped back the bile. I wanted a toy boy not a Chelsea pensioner.

'I don't want to hurry you,' I babbled, 'but I've got a driving lesson booked' handing him a towel. He cleaned up and struggled back into his damp shirt and relief overcame me as he looked more like Dave the u bend, and less like a pal of Ivy's from the day centre. Feeling guilty now I offered him a biscuit with the promised cup of tea, and, having cleared the blockage and re connected the pipes he cheerfully agreed. He chatted incessantly whilst drinking the tea and with my eyes closed, yes, he did sound twenty years younger but with the illusion spoiled as I visualized his chest reality came and bit me on the bum again.

'I'll pop the bill in the post,' he'd said as I showed him out.

Even the thought of my driving lesson couldn't shake me from my depression, and when Tina came round with a 'cooee' I answered with 'Oh hi, I don't think we'll bother today, I've had a bad morning.' She

49

was not to be put off however, and started shifting the furniture around. The settee was turned to face the window, and chairs lined up as rear seats. The cushions were placed on the floor and I was reminded that they were, in order - the clutch, accelerator and brake. My laundry basket lid became a steering wheel, the Hoover the gear stick and all that remained was for me to get in and start the engine. She patted the sofa encouragingly, and I sighed, obeying her command.

'Right' said Tina, 'Mirror, signal manoeuvre. Let's get this show on the road.' Before I'd got into first gear, she was complaining.

'You haven't put your seat belt on.'

'For God's sake Tina, it's only pretend you know?'

'Don't care,' she retorted, crossing her arms over her ample chest, feeling full of her own importance. 'That's a fail before you start in the real test.' Biting my tongue, I clipped the imaginary belt into its holder and turned the imaginary key. I pulled away and was startled when Tina suddenly fell backwards.

'A bit harsh on the old accelerator there my girl,' she gushed. I was beginning to regret asking my oldest friend, I guess it's only a step away from asking your husband to teach you? But with driving lessons so expensive I thought I could get a head start and then go onto - A1 guaranteed pass or your money back. BSM was £5 per hour more expensive! I couldn't believe how my lifelong friend and next-door neighbour could change so much when she put that clipboard in her hand. However, I decided to play the game, stopped the car, remembering the handbrake, opened the door, (the wooden airer). And that's another thing, how many people nowadays have to dry their smalls on a pre-war pink wooden airer that collapses every time the door opens, or the cat walks past or your husband sneezes. I want a tumble dryer!

'Where are you going?' asked Tina. 'I'm off to put some driving shoes on, these slippers are no good, and also, I think I need dual controls, so you can relax. I threw two more cushions to the ground. I hopped back in, seatbelt on, and revved the engine very loudly

'Lynda, you don't have to be that noisy, I know you're starting the engine.'

'It's a cold day, our Rover's always grotty on a cold day Dennis tells me, but then he says the modern cars are no better, and our car has gone round the clock once and still hasn't needed any major work, apart, that is, from a new radiator, three starter motors, water pump, carburettor......'

Tina interrupted, 'All right Lynda, can we go now?'

'Of course,' I smiled and stalled. 'Damn, that idiot in the garage doesn't know what he's doing. He couldn't service a Tonka toy, and he's gay, look at the way he keeps looking at me.'

'What are you on about now, Lynda – have you been drinking?' Tina was starting to lose her cool.

'I'm just repeating Dennis's opening sentence every time he gets into the car; he complains about the expertise of the mechanic then questions his sexuality. The car always starts eventually but then he spends that rest of the journey complaining about every other motorist on the road. Do you know he even phoned the Chief Constable once to complain about a Police car overtaking him, crossing the double white lines, even though it had sirens wailing and lights flashing?' Tina tried to ignore the desperate outpouring and get back onto safer territory.

'Well if he's talking about Mike at the garage, he's definitely not gay – every time I buy petrol I end up with oily fingerprints on my bum.

'Then why don't I?' I wailed. I answered my own question - as I often did, as no one in our house actually listens to me. I then shared with Tina my last experience of accompanying Dennis to the garage, describing Dennis's appearance. He had borrowed my razor, nicked himself several times and applied multi coloured quilted toilet tissue in several places. The effect was quite mesmerising, no wonder Mike the mechanic had seemed fascinated.

'Didn't you tell him,' asked Tina 'what he looked like?'

'What's the point; he still wears his flares and a jumper that was returned from Bosnia because no one there would wear it.' Tina shook her head and tried once more.

'Right let's go, we've been here nearly twenty minutes and we're still in the drive.'

'O K,' I agreed. 'Sainsbury's or down the market?' I pulled away.

'Nowhere,' giggled Tina, 'you've just hit the garage door, you should have reversed out onto the road.'

'Now that just not fair' I screeched at her; Dennis always backs it   in.

'Aah, but it was you who drove it last and you haven't learned reverse yet.' she said with glee.

At this point Mark came in and looked bewilderingly at the scene in front of him.

'Mum,' he started 'what on earth?'

'Get in, I'm learning to drive, and we don't have time to waste.' Obediently he climbed into the rear seat, Gran's ancient rocker.

'Mum, could your iron a shirt for me? I can't iron as well as you, oh, and could you drop it in later, not too late mind cos I'm off to the pub to meet the lads around eight?'

'I'm not sure I can concentrate with passengers.' I informed Mark. 'I'm half expecting your Gran to try to hitch a lift in a minute. I think we'll call it a day.' A sudden intake of breath from behind me made me stop and I looked over my shoulder at Mark, who had turned rather red and he spluttered apologetically

'Oh, I forgot to tell you, what with asking you to do the ironing and that, did you know Gran's half way down the road dressed in her nightie and slippers?'

'What do you think?' I answered, teeth gritted.

'Oh hell, she could be on the by-pass by now. Mark why didn't you stop her? It's these new tablets from the doctor -they're giving her delusions. Last night she was dancing with a plastic frog cushion, kissing him and telling us he was a Prince in disguise.'

'I think she was probably coming back though, she was heading this way,' he added as if that made it all right. Tina leapt to her feet.

'Come on, let's go and get her back, she won't be far away, her Zimmer Frame is still in the hall.' Tina was right about one thing, she wasn't far away, we found her on the central reservation, nightie pulled down to expose skinny wrinkled shoulders.

'Hello, I'm sunbathing,' she informed us. 'All I need now is a Bounty and a young semi-clad native to keep me company on my desert island.' I could only gasp and flap around like a landed fish but Tina saw the funny side.

'Oh, Ivy, this is a traffic island, there's no sand, no sea — come on home.' She winked at me, 'I think you'd better take her back to the doctors; these tablets are definitely too strong for her.' I remembered then why Tina was my best friend, she always looked on the bright side, and I returned her smile.

'Look,' said Ivy, the sun is setting and we stayed with her a moment to watch the warm orange glow, but she didn't seem to notice that it was flashing at regular intervals.

'Thank god she didn't go topless,' giggled Tina. The evening traffic passed us by, mercifully all the occupants far too wrapped up in their own thoughts to take much notice of three ladies linking arms and walking across the zebra crossing. A passing taxi driver did glance back as he had obviously noticed that the old dear in the middle was walking without her feet actually touching the ground, but he merely shrugged his shoulders and continued his journey.

We tucked her into bed, after crushing two sleeping tablets into her cocoa, and I put the chip pan on as Dennis was due home from his darts match. I also plonked the cushions back in their places, shifted the sofa back facing the television as there was boxing on tonight. Dennis has his routine you know, boxing means slippers, sausage and chips on his lap and a couple of beers followed by powerful snoring, often in perfect harmony with the oh so deaf one, leaving me the chance to write a couple of letters. I needed to find out as much as I could about my school friends and my replies were filled with questions about their lives, and very little about mine. But I was hoping and praying to have caught up with my past and have planned my future before D Day.

SEVEN

Aries: A project has distant goals but you're learning new things every day.

I turned, waving enthusiastically to Ivy as I left for work. Then I broke free my family and my responsibilities, tossing them aside like a used condom, and concentrated entirely on the new walk I was developing. I had watched Mandy at work, sliding through the workshops like a lioness stalking her prey, and had seen the lads suffering minor or occasionally major cuts from their various woodworking tools and I wanted to have this effect. With constant practise I felt I could empty the first aid box of plasters and small sterile bandages with my new wiggle. Sliding my hips into what I hoped was a suggestive position I took a deep breath   before stepping into the road. The screeching of brakes, a loud horn followed by a highly suggestive remark from a spotty white van driver had me scuttling back onto the pavement like a turkey avoiding a lunch date with Bernard Mathews. I don't know what upset me more, the fact that he had made me hop skip and jump or the fact that he had called me old - in fact an old tart. I decided a showdown would satisfy my anger, at being spoken to like that, at being forced to run, at just being my age and at my lost opportunities. He could take the rap for it all. I stood in front his bonnet and hands on hips stared at the windscreen.

56

'Get out the car.' I demanded and when our eyes met - he emerged.

'All right, keep your knickers on,' he jibed. I was relieved to see that he was no taller than your average twelve-year-old and built like a stick insect and I descended upon him, facing him squarely and within fiery breathing distance. His breath stank of cigarettes and his spots glowed.

'First of all, let me tell you that I am not a tart, and secondly that I am not old even though, I admitted, compared to you, having the intellect of a racing pigeon, I must seem it like it and thirdly and most importantly I do not wear knickers and I eat little boys like you for breakfast - O.K?'

'Yeah, right,' he squirmed; his shuffling feet obviously anxious to take him to the relative safety of his van. And, unable to return my gaze, he said 'right, I'll be off then.' As he drove away, wheels squealing, I felt the tensions of my little world float away and I prepared to do the walk again, soon all those men in despatch would have their tongues hanging out as I walked through.

'Hi,' said Cheryl, as I slunk into the office, 'oh no, have you put your back out? I warned you about doing it in a Fiesta, didn't I?' Momentarily I regretted my earlier conversation leading her to believe that I was conducting an affair with a second hand car salesman. But he had winked at me as we had passed the other day and said he'd see me at eight at the Cock and Bull. And my imagination had run away with me, fuelled by a gullible Cheryl.

'Yes, well perhaps it was a little ambitious,' I conceded, for I would far rather let her suppose I was doing it in a car rather than admit the truth.

'Well, who was it then, can't have been your Dennis, the original Bertie Basset?' asked Polly, and the girls all looked expectantly at me.

'I'm afraid that's for me to know and you to guess,' I replied fluttering my eyelashes.

'Spoil sport,' said Lorraine

'Meanie,' echoed Mandy. 'Give us a clue - was he handsome, under thirty and totally luscious?'

'Maybe.'

'Oh, nobody who works here then.' The girls giggled.

'I'll tell you all about him later,' said Cheryl, anxious to share her supposed knowledge with the girls.

'Nine o'clock- guess I'd better start working,' I said, turning on my computer. It still thrilled me to watch it kick into life and know that I was in control. I am Commander Lynda and it is my servant. I'd even left my sons behind with my expertise, and the World Wide Web was at my fingertips. Surely that would help me climb the ladder of success with the likes of Verity Osbourne Box and the rest? As I worked the girls whispered and nudged each other and, though twenty years their senior, I felt I had gained some respect from them, for sleeping around gave me incredible street cred. If they only knew. I reckon a sloth probably had a more eye-popping sex life than me. At lunch time we all sloped off to the visiting snack van and I chose my sandwiches. I still made Dennis's and didn't let on that mine came encased in nail breaking plastic triangles.

He would have told me what a terrible waste of money they were, and I already knew that, but for me it was just another measure of success.

'Prawns on a bed of wild lettuce on brown, today please.'

'Cheese and tomato,' said Cilla, 'how can you eat that stuff?'

'Yeah, same as Cilla's for me mate,' agreed Mandy 'I like proper English food.'

'But, hang on; you're all going out for Spaghetti Bolognese tonight?' I countered.

'Yeah,' said Mandy, looking at me strangely. 'Well, that's English innit?'

'I suppose so,' I agreed quickly, anxious to drop the conversation now. Sometimes these young girls got on my nerves.

We all sat in the car park on the small grassed area and the lads hung around hoping to see up skirts and as usual they were not disappointed for Cilla decided to sit cross legged as she could catch the crumbs better in her micro skirt. Her low-necked t shirt devoured all the excess however and she had to delve into her vast cleavage retrieving grated cheese, inviting all sorts of lewd remarks from Les and mates.

'You would think they'd get bored, wouldn't you, looking at my tits,' said Cilla loudly, clearly enjoying all the goggle-eyed looks and then exposed as much as she dare before gently brushing the wobbly mountains. Les licked his lips and swallowed hard, glad that his decency was ensured as he was still wearing his overlarge brown overalls.

59

'Come on lads,' said the foreman, 'the whistles gone — get back to work, leave these lovely ladies to stand up and adjust themselves in peace.' Of course, they all clocked in late that day. We sauntered back in, walking through the factory, the long way round, on the way up to the offices upstairs, and I always enjoyed the wolf whistles, even though it was the same every day. Sexual harassment, I can't get enough of it.

EIGHT

Aries: Sticking to routine leaves you feeling restless, but for now you must plod on.

It was Saturday again, how did they come round so fast? I swear that weekdays had been subject to budget cuts or something and were shorter. Maybe the three-day week had been re-introduced but I hadn't noticed. I lay in bed absorbing all those homely little sounds I knew so well. Dennis, a martyr to his adenoids, playing the trumpet voluntary beside me, opposites mangy dog howling to let indoors, and the oh so deaf one peeing in the pot beside her bed. I had long ago given up asking her to use the bathroom, fed up with the excuses that she force fed me on the rare occasions that I complained. For she was concerned that there might be an air raid (impossible) or a rampant spider (unlikely) waiting to attack her in the passage or, even worse, she might get chilblains from walking with no slippers on, because she couldn't find them in the dark (possible). Dennis refused to challenge his Mother, shrugging his shoulders, insisting that she was too old to change. *But she isn't old! That is not old. It's barely out of middle age.* But laying here today it suddenly occurred to me that she had been too old since we had married twenty-four and a bit years ago. And she was only sixty-four now; she might live for another twenty years yet, possibly even thirty. How old is the world's oldest woman? She might even live to one hundred and four! The realisation that my past might also be my future made me cringe and I curled into a ball pulling the quilted rose covered eiderdown high over my head.

'I want a duvet,' I complained to the slumbering Dennis, 'everybody I know has a duvet, except your Mother of course!' I prodded him with my elbow and he snorted loudly. He slid half-heartedly onto his side flinging an arm out, nearly garrotting me in the process. I had no option but to wriggle onto my side and he immediately curled his legs around me, patted my bottom as one does a friendly stray dog and whispered in my ear, burping last nights curried chips.

'H-h-happy Birthday, d-d do you want a cup of tea?' I just grunted and gritted my teeth because his next words were part of the daily ritual. 'Well you know where the kettle is, don't you?' Dennis hugged me violently, a movement which made me feel like a rugby ball in a scrum, snorted loudly, as he always did, then sighed deeply, ready to nod off again. He was not to know that I had spent my break yesterday at work viciously assaulting my calculator and had produced written evidence to demonstrate that he had said those words to me at least eight thousand times during our marriage and that was taking into account the nights I had spent in hospital producing our two sons and the occasional nights we had spent apart during away games with the football team. Would life after the menopause get better, would I stop being so sensitive, so easily upset? I left the marital bed, and slipped into something slinky, well actually my lemon candlewick dressing gown which was eminently suitable for covering a hot water tank and made me look like one as well. I met Ivy on the landing carrying her steaming chamber pot and she displayed a gummy smile, for her dentures were still grinning in the bathroom contained in a mug proudly announcing - a present from Morecambe. I smiled as I remembered Gary as a small boy asking why Grandma went all to way to Morecambe to buy her teeth.

'Happy Birthday dear,' she said patting me lightly on the shoulder before stroking my cheek quite gently. I was quite taken aback by this unusual display of affection for she was not a touchy, feely person. Normally her bony limbs were extended when a helping hand was needed. I acknowledged her greater need for the bathroom and headed for the kitchen - Dennis would eagerly be awaiting his cup of tea. I shrugged and laid the tray, dreaming of my plans to incorporate an ensuite. However, I did accept that I would probably have to encroach on next doors wardrobe to have the necessary space. Ours was not a house built for expansion. Dennis joined me for toast at the kitchen table some time later and presented me with a card. Hearts and flowers glared at me and I opened it gingerly, knowing that the sickly-sweet words would cause my teeth to grind. Why was I still here? - Because I was too cowardly to do anything else, that's why, and I hated myself a little more. It wasn't Dennis fault, or his mothers, it was mine.

I kissed his stubbly cheek.

'Thanks, it's lovely,' I lied. Dennis had added to the mindless prose - forty-four and you don't look a day over sixty ha ha, all my love, Dennis. Ivy produced her card, more hearts and flowers, but inside a pleasant surprise. Happy Valentine's Day it declared. Well, I suppose she'd remembered but probably, as usual, had gone to the shops without her glasses, still it was the first Valentine I had ever received so I stuck it up on the mantelpiece.

'Twenty-four years, Lynda, it seems hard to believe you were only fourteen when we first went out and just look at you now,' reminisced Dennis proudly. Fourteen! I thought, little more than a child, why didn't anyone stop me? But my Mum and Dad, bless them, had been too wrapped up in their own problems to cope with a lovesick teenager I suppose. And when their health failed them, they were probably happy to think that I was settled and being looked after when they could no longer do it. Yes, a husband trapped in a time warp, two sons cast in his mould and already metamorphosing, one daughter in law who in twenty years' time will be agonising, like me, over her wasted life, and a dotty old mother-in-law who at sixty four should still be agile, articulate and having fun - but wasn't and clearly never had been. *She is not old, it's like a mantra in my head. She is not old.* Not forgetting the toothless rabbit that I should enter in the Guinness Book of records for longevity. I mentally resolved to shoot myself at sixty-four if I was still living like this, no fifty-four probably.

'The boys will be across later,' explained Dennis 'and our Nita - we're having a bit of a do later, a surprise for you, a family meal at home, and I'll do the washing up, how about that then?'

'Lovely, smashing,' I replied. He's not all bad I thought, he is trying and I suppose I should too. I resolved to dress to kill and be nice to him all day.

'I'm off to shower Dennis, won't be long,' But even as I headed for the door, I was calculating how long I could linger in the bathroom, alone, dreaming my dreams.

'O.K love, oh, and I haven't bought you anything because I thought you'd like to choose something yourself.'

'Anything except you.' I muttered.

'What? Didn't hear you love.' Leaving my teacup on the drainer, I poked my head through the serving hatch.

'A fitted kitchen, a duvet to go in my new bedroom, a flashy red sports coupe, and the latest mobile phone to phone you from Paris, Rome and New York, or wherever.' Dennis and Ivy stared at each other, a pair of Marks and Sparks socks showed more spontaneity than those two and I fled to the bathroom, last decorated in 1983, when avocado had been the in colour. I could hear Simon and Emma or whoever they were on daytime telly downstairs telling me to have a brill weekend when I emerged from my bedroom feeling top to toe drop dead gorgeous with my newly painted nails, freshly washed and recently highlighted hair and underneath my jeans my body responded to pure silk slithering sensuously against me as I walked. My new silky cream top, a birthday present to myself, was all that covered my freshly moisturised and pampered skin and my hardened nipples brushed gently against the fabric. I sauntered into the kitchen where the table, blue and white checked cloth covered, solid wood 1950's style, displayed today's post. Dennis was

65

proudly holding a new brochure from a trendy D.I.Y chain.

'Look,' he informed me, 'there's our kitchen, I told you if you waited long enough it would come back into fashion!'

'There's nothing to beat a good wood,' added the oh so deaf one. 'Nowadays it's all that BSE stuff, it won't last you know!' she added knowingly. I refrained from trying to explain her confusion with M.D.F remembering just in time the lengthy argument with Mindless Mandy from the office who had insisted that BSE stood for British Standard of Excellence. The postman must have got a hernia carrying my post today.

'Are these all for me?' I asked, for usually Old Aunt Mabel was the only one who would fork out on a stamp, as she lived in Hastings. I spread them out as you would a pack of cards and felt a thrill at seeing all the brightly coloured envelopes sporting a variety of stamps some with greetings on the outside. I didn't know which to open first and in a sudden burst of childish enthusiasm plumped for eeenie, meenie, miney mo. My long, blushing pink nail landed on one postmarked Ontario and I was just about to pick it up when I became conscious of Dennis's eyes boring into me. He was standing behind his mother and I looked directly into his eyes trying to comprehend his wild gesticulations. He kept pointing alternately at my boobs then covering his chest and then, heeding my seemingly vacuous looks, placed both his outstretched fingers over his v-neck sleeveless sweater and shook his head violently.

'You've forgotten your bra,' he mouthed urgently. I chose however to return his worried stare, saying to his Mother, 'what's Dennis trying to tell me, do you know?' She turned to face him and he quickly ran his hands nonchalantly through his hair.

'N-nothing, n-nothing, I need a brush, that's all, open your cards, we all want to see them, d-don't we Mum?' A shiver ran down my spine, one of those that signals an urgent need for sex, and my nipples stiffened again. I thrust out my boobs, reaching for an envelope and Dennis looked at me with longing in his eyes. Unfortunately, I knew it was a longing to see me behave not a message meaning come here; I'm going to strip you naked on the kitchen table, and thrust my gift into your outstretched hands. I knew without a doubt that even if his mother had not been here his reaction would not have been any different and I sighed. The card was from Sally, who had at school the stature of one of those little Russian stacking dolls. She had worn national health pink specs in Primary School but was now, as the letter explained, jetting away with Richard Branson and obviously on a long-haul stopover judging by the postmark and unusual card saying I didn't know what. But her comments were readable. Hope you have a great day, don't do anything I wouldn't do, see you in August. Chow.

'Chow indeed.' And what does that mean when it's at home! I pictured her then, joining the mile-high club, and an envious moan escaped from my lips. The next one was from Verity Osbourne-Box, a personalised card which featured her holiday home, complete with chocolate box roses round the door and a large

Labrador basking in the sunshine. The only time our house had been photographed was for the local estate agents, (ideal first home, suit D. I Y enthusiasts and we all know what that means). And that was when they mistook the house number as well. Not that it mattered much, except that we didn't have double glazing, a porch or shrubs in tubs either side of the door. Yes, it did matter actually, it mattered about five thousand on the price as it happens! Wait a minute - I remembered it had also been featured on the telly, well two doors down had, Crimewatch, when our neighbour had been mistaken for a drug dealer and attacked. How anyone could confuse old Eddie, who lived in carpet slippers and carried a Tesco bag everywhere with an international drug baron was beyond me, but then I was a bit out of touch.

Julie had also written, a long letter enclosed in her card, a picture of a Humpty Dumpty type mound on the front, which proclaimed that I was over the hill. However, when I opened it up, I was reassured to see NO, you're just peaking, and a snow-covered Austrian type mountain with a naked female standing on the top gripping a pole topped with a fluttering Union Jack firmly between her legs. I tucked the letter in my jeans pocket to enjoy later and opened the remaining cards. All the girls at the office had sent one, even the boss. I lined them up on the mantelpiece leaving Dennis to answer the doorbell, which was merrily chiming out the usual inane speech that was guaranteed to make me consider attacking it with a hammer. Nice to see you – to see you nice it repeated. Dennis hummed as he shuffled along in his tartan woolly slippers to the door. He brought in Gary and Nita, his wife and Mark.

'Happy Birthday Mum, you look great,' said Mark. 'Might even take you down the pub later, introduce you as my girlfriend!'

'Not d-dressed like that you won't,' countered Dennis. Nita handed me some flowers.

'Tonight, it's your night, and we've all decided to all chip in and make your birthday special.' I had visions of a swift drink in the local, before going into town for a meal, and then perhaps onto a club, they did cater for the over nineteen's, didn't they?

'Brilliant,' I said.

'Yeah,' continued Gary, proudly, 'we're nipping to the Indian and bringing back a takeaway, so you won't even have to wash up afterwards.'

'Brilliant!' I repeated, though not quite with the same enthusiasm. Ivy sniffed loudly.

'And what am I going to eat then?' she held onto Nita, smoothing her sari.

'That's nice dear, but I'm not eating that foreign stuff, sorry Nita, but you know what I mean, don't you?' Nita knew only too well but ignored her comments as usual. If the truth be known she also preferred good old plain English cooking, which she had also been brought up on, as her parents who had left India in 1953 and had quickly adopted many of the local customs, all except religion and dress. Mother and Father had expressed their sadness at her marriage to Gary, but had not showed their displeasure at the wedding and welcomed the young couple to live with them until they could afford a house of their own. Gary thought this a brilliant idea and settled in immediately with his in-laws, resolving never to get enough money for a deposit.

Dennis laid the table that evening and had even bought party poppers, paper napkins, indoor fireworks and a bottle of Blue Nun for the occasion. I sat down surveying my family, reflecting on my life. Mother in law had taken out her rollers and although Dennis had felt unable to put his outdoor shoes on for the occasion his feet were firmly under the table so invisible. My sons, ever eager to bow to tradition, had brought their matching tartan slippers and completed the set. Nita looked gorgeous, so full of youth and I coveted her looks, I craved her chances. I speculated on her future but as I looked at the men clutching their pints, discussing football, my crystal ball refused to play, becoming murky and un-co-operative. My jealousy, of her and women in general, suddenly, and unexpectedly erupted and a deluge of misgivings, missed opportunities, and dissatisfaction clouded my mind momentarily. I turned from reluctant housewife to spitting viper and back again in the time it takes to microwave a plate of baked beans. The chrysanthemums looked lovely, though the choice of a milk jug as a container by the oh so deaf one should perhaps have been curbed. Nita dished out, Dennis provided the music, toe tapping line dance country ditties, and we all tucked in. As I had started on the sherry immediately after breakfast, I was feeling quite jolly and though Julie's letter had upset me another large glass of wine served to dull my memory. For Julie, as related in her letter, had just celebrated her birthday too and her husband had whisked her off to a dirty weekend in Bournemouth, leaving   her children with her ex-husband, who was under the illusion, she told me, that they were also his children. Julie and current partner had seen a show, gone to a casino and got absolutely plastered. She'd had a great time but did wonder why she had discovered in her handbag next day a black leather posing pouch. My handbag was more traditional, no exciting secrets, in fact at the moment it held Mother in Laws hearing aid, which I had forgotten to drop off at the Health Centre. Her recent trip to the hairdresser had seen Tracey, all mouth and scissors, cutting gaily, if somewhat recklessly. She was excited about her forthcoming wedding, or rather the hen night that would precede it, snipping through the lead to the earpiece, before applying a blue rinse She had then asked Ivy to shout when she had gone blue enough and although not getting a reply had gone on to do Mrs. Bailey whilst she was waiting. As Mrs Bailey had imparted much gossip which could be repeated for the afternoon clients Tracey had not kept an eye on the blue rinse, confident that Ivy would shout, and was completely unaware that Mediterranean Blue was the new colour developing. With the candlelight however this did not show too much and I did enjoy myself, until I passed out. At least I could tell my friends selected chunks to impress them, and Dennis giving me a fireman's lift to the bedroom would be one of them. His complaints about his back that followed would not. With the benefit of alcohol, I had enjoyed my forty-fourth birthday.   I slept soundly, snored loudly and, according to Dennis had explosive wind. All I could remember was requesting a Union Jack complete with flagpole as my birthday present.

NINE

Gemini: A partner being mysterious doesn't help, but the more you try to control a situation the more it slips from your grip.

Dennis, leaning heavily on his spade, toe poised ready for action, watched as I wiggled off down the road - off to my Feng Shui class tonight. Though it could do little more than broaden my understanding as my house, decorated circa 1963, needed more than a thoughtfully placed mirror and bundle of twigs to make it a place of calm, and serenity. The sitting incumbent was also watching me out of her bedroom window, shaking her head and more than likely clicking her dentures together in disapproval.

If I thought that he didn't care, or even notice the changes that were turning me from Mother Hubbard into a proud Model Y2K, as the girls in the office would say, I was mistaken. His brain was hurting with the unaccustomed effort of trying to find out how to stop me from wandering as he had convinced himself that was my intention. His mother, bless her, compounded his theories by sniffing my clothes loudly when I came in and commenting on the fact that I now changed my underwear, according to her, twice a day. She was also in the habit of pressing memory re-dial just, she hoped, to catch me out. Fortunately, so far, she had only connected to the Health centre, the water board and Nita, my daughter in law. I was tempted to direct her on one of those expensive chat lines but I could foresee a five-minute phone call punctuated by pardons and can you speak up and does that begin with an S? Followed by a huge bill, and a distraught young man giving up trying to spell the letters of masturbation, and having to resort to much simpler everyday phrases guaranteed to shock. I wonder why most common swear words are one syllable and generally only four letters long? Ivy's favourite was bugger which I know is longer but which she said frequently and with great gusto and obviously without knowing its meaning. Dennis preferred to ignore it and the boys still giggled when Gran said it- once even in church when she tripped over a raised slab which lay over poor Mr and Mrs Bates. Now they had been friends of Ivy in her youth, the local bakers, and when we had played Happy Families, we had nicknamed the bakers Bates and their son Master Bates, and Ivy had never understood our sniggering. 'They were a very nice family,' she would argue 'It wasn't their fault that they had been interned in the war - and their bread was lovely, and they always gave you a baker's dozen like a proper baker should do.'

As I reached the village hall it occurred to me that little had changed, my thoughts and aspirations were still basically focussed on home and family. Get a grip, I ordered myself, as I pushed firmly against the solid wood door which usually stuck, but today opened easily and extremely quickly. I entered the room; hands outstretched leaning far too far forward. After a couple of non-too dainty steps I was unable to recover my balance, falling to the floor before sliding almost gracefully along like a penguin slithering down an icy slope into the sea. I eventually stopped and found myself gazing at a pair of size 10's either side of my reclining body. I stretched to look upwards over my shoulder and followed the long jean covered legs right up to a bulging crotch. Looking past the crotch - eventually, I focussed on a black open necked shirt, then a captivating smile on a middle-aged man, handsome, chiselled features topped by dark closely cut hair. He looked into my eyes and spoke. His voice could have gravelled my front path.

'Nice to meet you, quite an entrance!' I blushed deeply, so deeply it started at my knees, and could only return his smile, feeling an attack of the hiccoughs coming. Not now please, I pleaded to my invisible friend. His hands stretched out to mine and I accepted his offer of help. I found my hands firmly trapped between his warm hairy paws and realised that my skirt was undeniably concertinaed around my waist. He looked down, this tall stranger and smiled,

'I guess you'll be needing your hands back' he said, staring unashamedly at my little red knickers. I tore my hands away and pulled my skirt quickly down to its rightful place

'Red suits you,' he laughed.

'Well I couldn't get much redder, could I?' I gushed.

I had never before felt so desirable, so sexy and life changing thoughts crowded my mind, my body, my very existence. My hopes and desires, suppressed for so long emerged in a jumble of expectations, grievances and lip-smacking desires. The rest of the evening the class discussed the practicalities and merits of rebuilding your house to catch the morning sun but mine passed in a haze of exotic, explicit dreams the like of which I had never experienced before. We didn't even sit together, the man in black and me and I didn't even risk a glance in his direction - but I was smitten.

The hardest thing was going home to Dennis; I walked along round shouldered, kicking small stones, sulking like a five-year-old. He was at the gate waiting for me still leaning on his spade. I bet he hadn't moved since I left. But Ivy stood in wait beside him and they were building up to something, I could see it, but I had no idea what was coming. He pulled open the gate.

'Come here,' he beckoned 'I've got a s-s-surprise for you.' The only surprise I wanted at this point was for Scotty to beam him, with the oh so deaf one, up and I found it hard to push my legs forward to go in the direction he was pushing me. Once inside I was unceremoniously thrust into the armchair and handed a pink candlewick blanket. I peered inside and a small face looked back at me, it mewed.

'It's a k-k-k-kitten,' said Dennis 'It's for you; it's a p-p-p-present.' I burst into tears, I sobbed, I held the kitten tight, and my heart was breaking.

'Oh, she likes it Dennis,' gushed Ivy and I cried some more.

TEN

Aries: It's time to let rip with your imagination.

The kitten demanded my attention and, in some ways, I did get to love it. Its mustard and cinnamon coloured stripy coat, three sizes too big, reminded me of American movies of the jailbirds who built the railroads. It skulked around with a permanent hang dog expression and I called him Des (short for Despair) but let Dennis believe that it was named after one of my favourite soap characters. I fed it when it howled for food, invited it onto my lap in the evenings where it purred loudly, relaxing nearly to the point of unconsciousness as I fondled it. But I was determined not to let it rule me as so many others had done in the past, and to that end I carried with me at all times a small water pistol which would blast poor Des when he attempted to climb the curtains or worse still my legs, or just generally irritated me. Perhaps, if I had trained Dennis to respond to this form of harassment, I would have been happier, though Dennis would inevitably have been suffering from colds and coughs, if not pneumonia, due to prolonged contact with water. My life was becoming fuller, my challenges more challenging and I was happier. The driving lessons were progressing, especially now that I skipped lunch on Wednesdays to keep my secret assignation with the man from All Pass Driving School. If I had hoped for romance there, which of course I had, I was disappointed. On the phone I had imagined a Dustin

Hoffman look alike but he had turned out to be a balding red head, of Humpty Dumpty proportions, whose hobby was collecting aircraft sick bags. If he'd had the benefit of the travel, I could perhaps have understood his enthusiasm however he only acquired them by writing off to various airlines that seemed bizarrely eager to indulge his hobby. But he was a patient man and a good teacher. Besides, as I was not yet at the stage of understanding how you could look in your mirror, indicate, change gear and negotiate a roundabout without hitting cyclists or pedestrians I needed all my concentration focused and romance was not an option.

I finished work on Monday, came home, prepared a meal, pushed it around the plate without enthusiasm, washed up, sorted Ivy's knitting pattern and ironed a couple of shirts. All I wanted to do now was dream, and wow, did I have a brilliant dream. My Feng Shui man featured prominently in many of my dreams and tonight was no exception as I collapsed into my chair, swiftly joined by Des. I lavished attention on the kitten, massaging him with long firm strokes, feeling his entire body tense then slacken echoing my movements. As my hand moved rhythmically the kitten seemed to double its length and I licked my lips and groaned, somehow sharing his ecstasy.

'Your back giving you problems is it?' enquired Dennis 'It's all this sitting at that computer thing you do now. You didn't suffer when you had a p-proper job, home cooking, hanging out the washing, and cleaning the bath and that did you?' He was, in a subtle way, of course, referring to the drop-in standards that he was experiencing due to my other commitments. He wasn't to know that I did clean the bath, but only before I got into it, and that the home cooking would soon reappear, albeit that it would be coming from someone else's home. My best friend, Tina, had decided that her future lay in providing this service professionally and as we were to be her 'guinea pigs' we would benefit from greatly reduced prices. And it was all going to be passed over the back wall, so I would even get authentic cooking smells. I wondered briefly if I could pass it off as my cooking, but that necessitated keeping the kitchen door shut and barricading the serving hatch and having nothing to do for about forty minutes except ponder my existence. If that were the case I might just as well cook myself. I decide to adopt the *here's one I made earlier approach* retrieving culinary delights from the freezer. It was then I spotted the oh so deaf one nodding knowingly, agreeing with her son, as of course, she always did, and I thought it best to go along with their assumptions. I looked almost longingly at Dennis and wondered if he wanted an early night. The theme tune for Footy Highlights blared out and Dennis leapt into action, grabbing his can and sat poised, waiting for the ten best goals of the month to be announced.

'Can I have a couple of sandwiches Lynda?' he pleaded, as the advertisements interrupted his programme. I stood up; inadvertently tipping the sleeping kitten off, whose automatic reaction was to claw desperately at my skirt. My finger was on the trigger within seconds and I fired, hitting the target spot on.

'Oy' yelped Dennis, 'I'm s-s-soaking.'

'Sorry, it was meant for the cat,' I apologised. 'I'll get your supper now.' Dennis mopped the trickling water from his neck with a cushion and grunted. The phone rang as I handed him his doorstep cheese and pickle wedges and I eagerly escaped into the hall. I answered it, settling into the deckchair which we used a telephone seat. Ivy argued that if you had a chair it was not common sense to only use it two months of the year and had insisted on it living indoors during inclement weather to ensure we got our money's worth. Mandy, from work, bubbled even over the phone and issued an invitation.

'Did I want to come to a party?' she said.

'What sort?' I inquired. But already I was thinking party frocks, one too many glasses of wine, scented candles and plenty of lonely men.

'No, not that kind of party' she replied, reading my mind. 'Tupperware tyre of party,' she giggled.

'Oh,' I groaned, 'That sort of party.'

'Well, not that sort of party exactly, but that's what you can tell Dennis, and the gorgon, it's really an Anne Summers party,' she explained. 'Could you escape?'

'Yes,' I informed her 'Of course, anything to get out the house.' I was still a little in the dark; who was this Anne Summers? Was she local? Is it arty crafty? And why would Mandy be going? It doesn't sound like her kind of thing. I wrote it on the board in the kitchen Tupperware party Tuesday, and circled it. I was ready for the 'Tupperware' party by seven, on the allotted day, an hour ahead of schedule, and sat outside in the yard enjoying a large glass of red in quiet anticipation

80

of the evening ahead. Tina had jumped at the chance of coming with me, having howled with laughter when I admitted that I had never heard of the lady in question.

'You won't believe the things you can buy Lynda,' she'd said to me with wide eyes and matching grin.

'Of course,' she said knowingly 'nobody ever uses them, but it's a real laugh.' I, however, had since been to work and got feedback from the office and now I wasn't so sure that these items were not in constant use in all these young girls' homes.

'We buy long life batteries in bulk,' explained Cheryl, 'on pay day - it works out so much cheaper.' But it was no substitute for the real thing, was it? The girls taunted me with tantalising morsels and insisted on making little buzzing noises in my ear.

Our patch of garden though small had a pocket-sized lawn, red brick walls and even a water feature. Next door's Tom Cat was skulking by the pond, showing a feint interest in the wildlife but I knew from experience that he had an assignation with Phoebe, the feline from two doors down with a grey powder puff coat and an enormous sex drive. Before I had finished my second glass of wine she had appeared, her tail held high, her nose in the air and that unmistakable come and get me look. I could learn from her, I thought. Tom, as he was aptly named, leapt on her within seconds and before she had a chance to stretch her long silky legs he'd done and he dumped her immediately. I knew just how she felt; Dennis was a Tom in disguise. For he snored loudly immediately after what he called his pleasure, which it obviously was, because it certainly wasn't mine. Not from what I'd heard recently anyway. Daydreams of my Feng Shui man surfaced with the sudden burst of sunshine for he had smiled at me again last week even venturing a small wave from his seat in the back row of our class. I wanted to be more like Phoebe and advance on him but once I had stuck my claws in I wouldn't him let him go so easily. Besides Cheryl had warned me that as he hadn't made his move and I'd been in the same room with him twice he was definitely married or gay or both. The doorbell went and I went through the back room to meet Tina as she slid into the kitchen. She advanced towards me with a huge smile and a Tower of Pisa lean. If the walls had not provided her with support she would have been on the floor by now.

'Tina, what are you like? You're absolutely plastered and we're not even there yet.'

'You have to get yourself in the mood, for all those games you play, I couldn't do it sober,' came the slurred reply. I was having second thoughts; would I be able to cope or would I be too embarrassed? I threw down a third glass of wine in one hit. No - Nita, my so shy daughter in law, had said she'd come too, as she'd had so much fun last time she went. It couldn't be that bad, could it? I jumped as the doorbell rang again.

'Hi,' called Nita, 'Ready for it are you?' she giggled. She too showed signs of inebriation and I wondered how we were all going to reach our destination as my head was now feeling rather remote from my legs. Oh well, go for it as the girls would say. You only live once, and that was my aim wasn't it?

'Everybody ready?' I shouted, pushing them along what we lovingly called the back passage, and then Ivy materialised, the spitting image of Dame Edna Everage, minus the gladiolas, from the front room.

'I'm ready,' she said, 'Do I need a hat?' Three startled faces looked at Ivy in disbelief and I implored my brain to think up a quick no you can't because reply but the goldfish in me just kept mouthing think bubbles.

'It's been years since I went to a Tupperware party, but I don't suppose they have much new do you, there's only so much you can do with a sandwich box isn't there?'

'Come on,' encouraged the inebriated Tina, 'give her a brandy and we'll be off.' More luck than judgement got us to the host's pretty semi in Dimsdale Avenue and I herded everyone in and pushed them into chairs. The oh so deaf one I propelled into a corner and apologised to her once again about how sorry I was not to have picked up her hearing aid.

'We'll start with a game,' said the hostess.

'We need two teams, who's going to be team leader?' Ivy raised her hand, with reckless brandy induced confidence, her ability to lip read unfortunately intact.

'Stand here,' said the hostess, put this penny tight between your knees (she giggled) and walk across the floor before dropping it into the top of this milk bottle. Incredibly we all heard the tinkle as the coin dropped in. Try as we might no one else that night succeeded in that game. Ivy was over the moon. Apparently, some girls can hold it tightly rather higher up but we were not that drunk! A fat black suitcase appeared on the floor when we had all been given a glass of cheap plonk and

I glanced nervously at Ivy, but she was seemingly as eager as me to examine the contents. We had already glimpsed the colourful pictures in the catalogue but it did not prepare me for the hands-on experience. The room lit up like Christmas with sex toys buzzing, throbbing, with day glo lights, flashing lights and the biggest condoms I had ever seen.

'Oh my God, they're edible,' screeched Cheryl. I looked at Ivy in the corner, large glass of red wine in one hand - an absolutely enormous vibrating black man's willy in the other. I gulped. She had slipped on, albeit over her day clothes, the French maid's outfit.

'How about that for stirring your tea?' she shouted across the room, waving the throbbing object gaily over her head. Please let Dennis be asleep when we get home, I prayed. I filled in my order sheet surreptitiously, hand shaking, words flooding like a tidal river with endless tributaries across the page. I ordered a vibrator, carefully adhering to the instructions for choosing - see if it feels good on the tip of your tongue. I decided on small (which still looked enormous, compared to you know who). I ticked the box for handbag size, wondering how many women are so desperate that they can't wait till they get home, or am I the one with a negligible sex drive. I started to feel slightly depressed at this thought so also ordered a jelly willy stress buster. After another glass of mediocre wine and a chocolate willy topped with hazel nuts, we all crawled home. Ivy didn't seem to need her Zimmer frame that night, she had quite a jaunty step - perhaps it was the company, I thought. She also sniggered continuously but when we reached our door all was quiet and we sneaked in like a pair of schoolgirls arriving back after lights out.

ELEVEN

Aries: Pander to your whims and flaunt that sexier image.

Ivy seemed none the worst for her adventure and I sensed closeness, a new–found bond, with Nita that had previously been missing from our relationship. We had gone from the mother-in-law/daughter–in–law to a rather intimate togetherness. She confessed that she'd cast me as 'Mrs Average-but-Boring,' but had rapidly elevated me to Mrs Knowing and probably Enjoying after the Tupperware Experience. Engaging various techniques, but without actually asking me, she tried to find out what I'd ordered but I would only, with a knowing wink, admit to reserving a new lunch box. Three weeks seemed a long time to wait for delivery but it did give me ample time to look for a suitable hiding place. I dug out and replanted the small rockery, leaving a small letter box shaped and sized space at the back, away from prying eyes, but quite accessible if you knew where to look for it. My new colourful annuals stood proud and moist, revelling in their perfect environment. Dennis was quite impressed that I now had time to garden as well as keep up all my other new found hobbies. If he only knew. I also realised that I had overlooked the fact that feeling randy might involve me in moonlight excursions in dubious weather conditions clutching a small spade. I had a few nagging doubts, with the filming for this documentary looming ever closer, about the secrets that this would divulge to the world in general, and my family in particular. Having tried so hard to re–invent myself   I was now considering the impact it may have on my family. Who would have thought it, me, Lynda Fisher, a femme fatale? Well maybe not yet but who knows?   My regrets being that I yearned for the figure of a model, the brains of a news reader and my age divided by two.

'Hell, that's a lot of wishes, girl,' I said aloud, sighing deeply absentmindedly stroking Des. But despite my misgivings the prospect of divulging my life was rather exciting and my body tingled with anticipation.

'Dennis,' I called out, 'Fancy an evening at the Swan, do you?' He looked at me sideways, obviously sensing my intentions, and said 'O.K a quick one, but my backs playing up, I'll tell you now'. That was his subtle code for no sex tonight and I wondered if it was worth dousing myself in French perfume and squeezing into my new Prussian blue lacy Basque and fastening my 10 denier sheer stockings.

'Oh, sod it, you never know who you'll meet do you, and I can always dream can't I?' The evening passed more or less uneventfully but I was delighted by the remarks of Dennis's work mates about my new figure and their lip licking reactions when Dennis just had to tell them that it was my new fancy underwear holding me in. Consuming three pints in quick succession gave him another excuse to avoid sex and the confidence to talk loudly about things he couldn't understand - like me. Most men, I thought, may have had a quiet word with their doctor or started reading the women's problem page but Dennis could only express himself in the pub, crudely and loudly.

'She's got those s-s-s-stays on you know- like my Gran used to wear, holds her bits together, and she can hardly breathe, but she don't seem to m-m-m-m-m mind. And me mother laughs - says the Victorians have come back to our house.'

'No Dennis, it's not like your Gran wore, or anything like your mother wears, it's fashion,' I explained through gritted teeth, blood rushing to my cheeks. The lads, unlike Dennis, obviously appreciated the thought of my encased yet curiously exposed body and I made damn sure that they knew that stockings had also made a comeback. By the time I got home I was wishing like hell that my 'Tupperware' had arrived, but Dennis just wanted his cocoa. I went to bed that night, feeling cheated and had to content myself with dreaming about the new locum at the surgery where Ivy had a frequent visitor pass. I bet that professional men appreciate their wives, well, you only had to look at the doctor's wife and the locums too - they always looked smart and wore wrap around smiles - it must mean they are having great sex.

Nita joined me for coffee when the big boys had gone off to football on Saturday afternoon, and we had a real heart to heart. Well, her heart anyway, because I wasn't ready to share mine with anyone, yet.

'Gary wants to start a family, while we're still young,' she explained.

'But you're not so sure, are you?' I pumped her, trying to tease out her innermost thoughts. I was conscious of our improved relationship, for several months ago she would never have confided in me like this, and my spirits rose.

'Well, I can see the sense in it you know,' she continued dunking her chocolate biscuit, 'and my family think it's a good idea, and Gary says well, you did it, so it's got to be good hasn't it? But - Oh Lynda, I'm not so sure, I mean I don't want to end up like you, do I?'

TWELVE

Aries: You're not the type to live dangerously so look out.

It was a bad start to the day. I overslept. Then I discovered the rabbit had gone AWOL. A nail-biting search revealed him hiding under the tender green lettuces, and a quick prod revealed he was still very much alive. Arriving at my sanctuary, I found the office buzzing – not with work related stuff obviously. I ditched my insecurity along with my ankle breaking, toe pinching shoes. Perched on my typists' chair slowly swivelling from side to side I brooded on the subject of comfort versus chic. Chic won, obviously. My push them up, thrust them out bra had obviously been wired with barbs and I squirmed, nudging my boobs hopefully inconspicuously, endeavouring to get them to nest comfortably. My just above the knee skirt had developed a dangerous habit of slithering up to my thighs and was now allowing my stocking tops to peep out. Mandy, in her usual subtle way was standing legs apart in the middle of the floor with her hand up her skirt adjusting her underwear.

'Who the bloody hell invented thongs?' she complained

'It's got to be a man, hasn't it?' I hummed agreement as mine, though it definitely awakened responses in my body, was about as comfy as sitting on cheese wire. If I were to find myself on a desert island it would no doubt be a useful and indispensable tool. I

90

decided to slip to the restroom at coffee time to make the necessary adjustments. Mandy let out a loud Aah of relief and promptly sniffed her hand.

'There's no mistaking the smell of sex, is there girls?' she giggled. Lorraine turned to protest.

'Didn't you shower before you came to work, you dirty cow?'

'Yes, I did, actually, but then I stopped off in the bus shelter with Malcolm for a quickie, thought it would set me up for the day.'

'Malcolm?' the words squeaked out from my mouth before my brain engaged fully, 'that lad from despatch?'

'Yeah, so?' said Mandy, now clearly on the defensive.

Lolly joined in, fighting my corner unexpectedly

'I just thought that you didn't want to be a notch on his bed post, that's all,' she sniffed.

'I'm not,' she retaliated 'He's a notch on the bus timetable.'

'Post girls,' shouted Malcolm as he came in pushing ahead of him the squeaky tea trolley. His tongue was stuck out, as he concentrated on controlling the wobbly wheels

'Tea, coffee sticky buns & raspberry condoms.' He was used to us all totally ignoring him and a little taken aback when he found six open mouthed girls staring at him. I bet he hadn't even started shaving yet? He probably still goes for half price on the bus - yet Mandy had ravished him! I couldn't understand it, nor dare I say it, the younger generation in total. Although I have to admit that I had sex before we were married, we had been engaged. I smiled as I remembered the weekend away, Brighton - Sea View Hotel, although not from our room which overlooked the park - the car park. A Woolworth's brass wedding ring burning my finger, guilt engraved in my fixed smile, emitting nervous high-pitched giggles. My Dad thought I'd gone with the Church Youth Group to Pontypool and I was terrified he would discover the truth. Dennis had told his Mother that he was off to watch an away football game, something he often did. Our first night together had been a disaster, all that fumbling, shyness and embarrassment. I had never before seen Dennis without his socks and I found his feet difficult to accept. Long knurled yellow nails on the end of white, almost, dare I say it, webbed feet, which had previously been covered in Bri-Nylon were sticking out from the legs of his blue striped pyjamas. I had the awful feeling their appearance would be matched by an equally awful odour. I had taken advantage of Dennis going off to brush his teeth in the shared bathroom and hopped into bed still wearing white bra and panties. I cringed as I remembered that the first night, despite obvious deep longings, they had remained firmly in place — a chastity belt could not have done more. We were both eager to get home and from then on settled with kisses and cuddles on his Mums sofa until we married. And now, I shook my head, disbelievingly, they talked about it all the time, did it all the time and obviously thought about it the rest of the time. I wasn't sure whether to be disgusted or plain jealous. A bit of everything maybe.

Mandy was first to the trolley and she grabbed a lengthy iced bun and slid it suggestively between her glossy lips.

'Hi,' she drawled.

'Didn't I tell you earlier never to talk with your mouth full?' Malcolm leered. 'Anyone else want one of my nine-inch fancies while I'm here?' Although hotly embarrassed I was absolutely fascinated by these open displays of sexuality. I jumped as Malcolm caught my flushed, rapidly blinking gaze.

'Hello there, Lynda, lovely Lynda, when are you coming for a ride on my fork lift?' he enquired, thrusting his hips suggestively in my direction. I heard myself snigger like someone from a Carry On film and bit my lip. Pull yourself together girl, you're not a sex mad adolescent, and he's not old enough to ride a moped.

'Got to get on,' he continued, after his seemingly X ray eyes had examined me from head to foot. Lorraine licked her lips, watching his retreating bum,

'Wow, gives you damp knickers don't it girls. I'm definitely going to his twenty first next week. You coming along Lynda?'

My 'maybe' got lost in the chorus of you bets from the other girls and at around ten past ten we settled down to start work. At lunchtime I shot off to have another driving lesson, my test was coming up fast and I was determined to pass first time. Then all that remained would be to tell Dennis, but I'd get over that hurdle when I came to it. I was finding it hard to keep up with the housework, as my hectic lunchtimes were exhausting me. When I got home all I wanted to do was

93

collapse onto the sofa. On Mondays I was taking swimming lessons. The instructor Simon was very attentive and as my fear had been extreme, he was content to paddle along beside me as I struggled to stay afloat. As I obediently floated on my back gently waving my feet, he would hold me firmly under my neck and his glistening body had me enthralled. I guess it was all that life saving and diving that gave him such a sleek muscular body and I suppose he used his staff discount to sit in the tanning lounge every day. I speculated on the possibility of wearing a bikini at my age, or even half a one if I got to go abroad on holiday, which was my next ambition. On Monday evening I was taking conversational French at night class and found the rhythmic chanting of French verbs with Jean Pierre captivating and his accent most enjoyable. I may not be having sex like my young friends but I was most certainly becoming obsessed with it. Dennis decided that my interest in lovemaking was entirely due to a lack of physical chores like ironing and vacuuming and even offered to decorate the house in an effort to inspire my interest in all things domestic. You'd think he'd be glad that I wanted his body wouldn't you, but he wasn't and if I'm honest I didn't but it was a step too far to commit adultery in my world.

THIRTEEN

Aries: When it comes to life, take a look at the bigger picture, don't settle for the mundane.

As I came downstairs to start another day the front door coughed out a brown envelope through the letter box and I rushed to retrieve it from the almost bald coir mat before the kitten used it as a porta loo. Dennis had insisted on training it on newspaper despite my protestations that there were wonderful new inventions like cat litter and dirt trays.

'Never had them in my day,' he quoted, in his like old father time voice, before retreating back behind his Daily Mirror, nose twitching, trying hard to ignore the yellow damp patch and the pungent odour now emanating from the sports page – and spreading! Private and confidential Lynda Fisher, it stated. Puzzled, I turned it over but there was no identifying mark, just a blob of a red circle which may once have been a postmark. I propped it against my Emmaline Pankhurst pepper pot while I made the coffee and toast but eventually curiosity got the better of me. Correspondence addressed directly to me was still quite a novelty but the brown was a little off-putting. I remembered that Dennis filed all his buff envelopes under the plump cushion on the sofa, saying that if it was important, they would write again. When the pile got too large and the oh so deaf one's little legs could no longer reach the ground due to the increased height of the furniture Dennis would retrieve them moodily and relocate them in the pigeon shed where they would provide a warm lining in the boxes. A clipped bundle of white A4 sheets fell out when I opened the envelope and a yellow sticky note floated onto my lap.

Hi Lynda, just a little questionnaire for the prog. Fill in as much as you can but you are allowed to leave out the parts that may be embarrassing (but I'd like to know anyway). Ignore questions that may incriminate you in a court of law. Nudge nudge. Lots of love Verity.

Having grabbed a biro, I chewed on the top for a moment considering whether to put off replying until I had a fountain pen. Verity always wrote in green italics. I ditched the biro but opted instead for a pencil so I could correct and amend as I went before totally committing to writing my abridged autobiography. Having skimmed the first page I relaxed a little, it looked fairly innocuous. Question 1. How many times have you been married? So far so good. Question 2. How many men have you slept with? Verity's green hand writing had crept in commenting (That also includes men who were far too exciting to sleep with, if you know what I mean!) Question 3. How many affairs have you had? NO, it wasn't going to be that easy, as it was now time to commit virtual adultery, or admit to a sad boring life. I flung it to one side; I may as well fill in the happy ever after version and let her think I was Snow Bloody-White. If she didn't believe in fairy tales, she would think I was lying. If she did believe and I told the truth she would be watching for my nose to get longer. Maybe the truth would work. A loud screeching from upstairs disturbed my thoughts.

'Lynda, are you there?'

'Yes, I do believe,' I replied, looking for the magic fairy. But I can hear the wicked witch of the north, banging her stick. Now, if this was make-believe, I could wave my magic wand and she would disappear in a puff of smoke. However, reality made me head for the passage. I called back wearily

'Coming.' As I climbed the stairs, I thought of all the possible reasons that she could demand my attention. I hoped it was not because the kitten had fallen into the chamber pot again. No - it was O.K - Des was lying in his usual place across the top stair where he could be sure of endangering the lives of all who crossed his path. And sure enough, as I approached, he extended his claws   narrowing his eyes in readiness. I tried smiling, murmuring sweet nothings and put out a hand to stroke him but he was a kitten with attitude, prickly as a hedgehog. I quickly withdrew my hand and took a massive step over him suffering only minor damage to one ankle, with the   merest whisper of blood. I looked back at him. I wanted to love him, enjoy his plump little body curled up on mine and listen to his purring but he just wanted to pick a fight. Ivy repeated her banging even more vigorously

'I'm coming,' I exploded.

'You're touchy,' moaned the oh so deaf one, who was balanced precariously on the side of her bed. My lips parted leaving my teeth firmly knitted together.

'Yes, mother, what can I do for you?'

'I seem to have both my legs down one leg of my cotton interlock knickers and I tried pushing my stick inside to get one leg out and now that's stuck as well.' I slipped on to my knees and cautiously pushed back her Crimpelene skirt.

'Yes, Mother you are in a bit of a pickle, aren't you?' I chuckled. I peered inside the cavernous white garment and dipped in a hand to retrieve the walking stick, two hankies and a ball of wool. I decided, having glanced at her weary eyes staring into outer space, that I should not ask questions. With all the aplomb of Paul Daniels I then rescued her skinny legs. I just couldn't see Verity having to deal with situations like this but to be honest my tension slid away as I giggled at her predicament. I needed light relief and this was as good as it gets in my house. My period was a week late and I'd been reliably informed by Mandy, big boobs and false eyelashes, that the end was nigh. I hadn't expected the change to come this early but knowing my luck it probably was and I wasn't ready for it. I didn't want it, and I was going to fight it. I was only forty-three and not prepared to go downhill, not like this, on a bob sleigh. I refuse to miss my chance at life, let the figure slide, develop a crinkly bottom which would slowly but surely creep down my legs like Mount Vesuvius on a good day and have no chance of attracting anything other than a short sighted, hearing impaired widower who needed a good spring clean. I looked closely at Ivy who I'd now dressed more appropriately. She was only seventy-four but I'd seen eighty-year olds with more style and energy. I made up my mind that I was going to break with tradition and grow old disgracefully. I'd do a Dolly Parton, well, to a degree. I couldn't imagine Dennis being confronted by a dizzy blonde with melons for boobs and make up by Polyfilla; he'd probably take to his bed with a hot water bottle over his privates.

FOURTEEN

Aries: Give yourself a break, ease off the domestic strife. The sex goddess Venus is demanding your attention.

Miss Butterworth singled me out for attention.
'Can you type this up before you go to lunch please Mrs Fisher?' My workmates, of course, were typing furiously, keeping their heads down for The Spotted Dick got very crowded at lunchtime

Yes, of course,' I replied, but I had more pressing things on my mind than banging out a quote for a dining room suite in oak with matching sideboard. I slid the copy into my tray heaving a sigh, chasing the sympathy vote. Cheryl rushed to comfort me, 'It's only a driving test Lynda, and you've had the lessons, now just go out there and drive. No problem!' Lolly, suggested her recommended approach, which was rather predictably, - 'No bra, short skirt - pout a lot.' She then blew a giant bubble with her seemingly everlasting gum and thrust her ample chest at the top drawer of the filing cabinet successfully enabling it to shut with a whoosh without ruining her iridescent orange nails. If I had looked like her that would have been my number one plan. I was chasing dreams but reality kept biting my bum and that theory test pass that I'd been so chuffed with wasn't doing a lot for me now - being that I had hidden it in the lining of my everyday handbag. If only I could take the test on a Game boy I would pass, I know it, but the prospect of facing a real live examiner and having total control of a feisty little red Fiesta scared me to death. I wished I'd booked up before my body had so unexpectedly gone to seed. Plan two drifted into my mind. If I could be mildly inebriated when I took my test my confidence would surge. I would be able to reverse around corners without hitting a lamp post and maybe even give the examiner a blow job whilst doing a three-point turn. Oh God - was this me talking? I sounded more like Mandy every day - I would have to lay off the Bacardi Breezers. I fished in my handbag retrieving my mouth spray and squirted it liberally. Cheryl couldn't believe that I'd managed without one all these years.

'You're clutching at straws now,' laughed Polly – 'you haven't had a drink since yesterday lunch time.' Cheryl patted her nose 'Aah, well perhaps she needs to get rid of the taste of something else. I saw you walking in with Les this morning, and your lipstick has definitely lost its gloss.' She elbowed Lolly, Les's sister, in her usual brutal way, leaving Lorraine coughing, nursing her soon to be bruised body after its unexpected encounter with the wall.

'Don't be so stupid,' I snapped, 'Les is barely out of school uniform.'

'Yeah, you've got a point,' sniggered Cheryl, 'I prefer them in it, don't you?' The alarm I had set on my computer screeched at me that it was time to go, death row awaited. I decided then and there that if I couldn't pass my driving test, I would give it all up, and go back to being a sad middle-aged wife and mother, but I held my head high as I trudged past the girls who all wished me good luck. I would have to suffer the wrath of Miss Butterworth's neglected work when I returned.

My instructor, waiting outside by the car with five-foot-long L plates front, rear and top, looked me up and down, and I felt that the clothes I had chosen - fawn slacks and a loose fitting demure white blouse probably gave the right impression. I could still only drive in flatties and so I slunk rather than slid into the car. At least I had my lucky knickers on. Not that they had been lucky so far but well, you never know do you, and I would not be caught out if and when I decided to live life to the full. You wouldn't catch me in white high legs any more. The sick bag collector dropped me off with minutes to spare, less time to worry he said, and then he wished me luck, he didn't add that I needed it, but on the other hand he didn't say I didn't need it - bastard. OOPS there I went again; Cilla and Mandy had infiltrating my mind and left their less attractive habits with me. As I stood on that cold blustery corner watching a man with matching clipboard hopping over to me, chin thrust forward, the immortal words of my instructor wafted depressingly over me. When I had held the wheel for the very first time he had simpered, 'You need one hour's lesson for every year of your life.' That little phrase had nearly ended my driving career then and there as I did a rough calculation.

'Good morning,' the examiner shouted at me and I stared back at him wondering if he had said that already and I'd been alone and lost and had not heard. What a great start I thought. I assumed the pose and pasted what I hoped was a confident smile on my face. My dry mouth caused my lips to part and stick firmly against my teeth and I grinned an unstoppable grin. My Fen Shui man smiled back, a professional smile.

'Let's make a start shall we Mrs Fisher?' Lucky knickers or not they wouldn't be seeing the light of day today, he'd never told me what his job was, or was it a career? But I hadn't asked him, had I? I'd only ever talked about, well nothing really, I didn't even know if he was married with children, or if he had a dog? After several fumbled attempts at putting the key in the ignition the car kicked into life. Mirror signal manoeuvre.

'We're going to the end of this road and then we're turning right, please go when you're ready.' My right leg met the accelerator and started to jiggle, should I put on the radio hoping for Riverdance, would that reassure my examiner? I inhaled, exhaled loudly and placed my right hand firmly on my leg. Unfortunately, my entire left side then responded with knee jerking severity. I watched it wobble and writhe and felt an urgent need to leave the car right now but, of course, I couldn't because jellies can't walk, can they? Any minute now and I'd be disco dancing. Under my breath I repeated 'Shit shit shit.' Well, I think it was under my breath.

'When you're ready,' Fen Shui repeated slightly louder this time.

'OK,' I squeaked bravely setting off down Harold Wilson Avenue. At least I'd set off with the examiner which was more than my friend Sue, who had had such a bout of nerves that she had belted off down the road leaving the examiner foot poised and open mouthed on the pavement. She had failed before he got in. I gave a

103

little yelp as I remembered suddenly who was sat beside me and I risked a glance as I turned left. Yes, it was him all right, still tanned from his recent trip to somewhere obviously quite hot. I breathed in his aftershave, admiring his relaxed hand clutching his clipboard. His eyes looked dark and inviting - almost Egyptian, I'd be his Cleopatra any day.

'Straight across the roundabout.' My emergency stop almost put him through the windscreen; the fire engine had appeared out of nowhere and hurtled across my path. Thank goodness for seat belts.

'You won't be required to do another emergency stop today,' he soothed me after a moment's reflection, 'please continue now.' A drop of rain from a passing cloud took refuge on my windscreen followed almost immediately by hail the size of golf balls and despite my urgent thought waves the windscreen washers refused to turn on. I felt a hot flush surging through me.

'Damn the change - not now,' I demanded 'Sorry,' I said, 'talking to the rain.' I explained. My fingers tickled every button I could reach without abandoning the steering wheel and somehow, they started up, I hoped to god that the rain wouldn't stop again as I had no idea how to turn them off now. What seemed like a fortnight later came the words I was waiting for,

'I am pleased to tell you.'

'Oh God I love you,' it slipped out before I could stop it.

'Can I kiss you?'

'I love my job sometimes,' he smiled. He passed me a piece of paper and he was gone. A tap on the windscreen and Mr Sick-Bag peered at me.

'I'll drive you back Lynda. The more successful I am the more customers I lose,' he crowed. 'Doesn't make sense does it?' And I had to go home to Dennis; would he share his four wheels? Would England win the World again? Time to ponder!

FIFTEEN

Gemini: A relationship isn't what it used to be – forget your past ways.

Thursdays was bingo night at the Regal and Dennis always dropped his Mum off there before escaping to the Kings Arms to sit with all the other men who were providing a similar taxi service. In the past I had accompanied Ivy, when my perfume had filled the car which would then cling reassuringly to his shirt. But now I preferred to walk briskly to my Fen Shui class leaving Dennis to breathe in a curious mixture of mothballs, Parma Violets and stale toilet water. His pal, Fred, his enormous frame overhanging a bar stool, was waiting as usual and he passed Dennis a Guinness before sucking the overflowing froth from between his podgy fingers. Dennis had seemed very downhearted lately and Fred determined not to sympathise less he became burdened with all his problems. He had a bucketful of his own being married to Irene, the biggest nagger in the Western Hemisphere.

'Cheers Dennis,' he quipped as he braved a clinking of glasses. Dennis looked down as most of his pint landed on his lap, and sighed.

'Sorry mate, I'll get you another,' said Fred beckoning his request to the barman. Fred's mind was awhirl with the subjects that he knew he should not mention tonight for fear of further depressing his morose drinking pal. Bristol Wanderers had lost last Saturday, a crushing defeat, and although Fred could see the funny side of it, the funny side being that the team had hidden in the changing rooms until the ground had been cleared of angry fans, he knew that Dennis would not. He wondered momentarily if they were still there, munching crisps, surviving on canned lager. If they were, they'd be clean though, he thought, because there was always a nice hot tub. Wandering Wanderers - he could see the headline in the Bristol Evening Post now. Dennis had marched home that night alongside Fred, bursting with resentment, and Fred had witnessed Dennis's size nines ramming home the gate against a particularly rampant bush with evil thorns which had, admittedly, been annoying Dennis for weeks. As the gates hinge gave way Dennis had removed his red and white striped scarf, wound it round the post and gate pulling it tight, stretching it ruthlessly. Fred had lumbered off as fast as he could and spent his lunchtime next day asking discreet questions of his mates hoping to find out what was bugging the normally placid Dennis.

'Woman trouble,' had been the reply, but Fred, having known Dennis and Lynda for twenty-five years, shook his head telling them they were barking up the wrong tree this time.

'I went to their wedding I did, it was a marriage made in heaven.' Their replies, though mixed in content, had all amounted to the same thing, it was bound to be a woman's fault at the end of it, and it always was — cos women had changed, they had too many rights, and they didn't do as they were told any more. Fred didn't like to admit that his wife Iris, aka Attila, had never been what you might call a model wife, more like a cross between Hitler and Germaine Greer. But then, he sighed, he wasn't so much of a catch himself, was he?

'You're quiet tonight,' said Dennis 'that wife of yours giving you gip, is she?'

'When isn't she? I'm having it put on my grave Dennis - nagged to death and beyond I shouldn't wonder,' he sighed, before changing the subject to something he hoped more positive.

'How your boys? They're big lads now - the spitting image of you Dennis. I saw your Gary down the chippy the other day.'

'That's cos Nita's won't make him chips, says they're bad for him. See what I mean? Always causing tribulations they are.'

'Oh, sorry to hear that Dennis, but then she likes curries and that doesn't she, being foreign like?'

'Yes, Fred, but you can't eat them every day, can you? It's not natural. It's not like your staple diet is it?' Dennis was also trying to get off difficult subjects and turned to racing.

'What's running in the 2.30 tomorrow then?' he asked Fred hoping he would give him a hot tip.

'I keep hoping my wife will do a runner, but each morning I wake up to a face like a left-over pancake staring at me, and god does she nag, you don't know how lucky you are Dennis.' Dennis took the bait and started to elaborate over his marital issues.

'Lynda used to nag, but she doesn't even have time to talk to me now, she's that busy getting herself all tarted up for work. Do you know that sometimes I even have to make my own sandwiches?'

'Well I do mine Dennis - out of choice, I'm sure my wife's trying to poison me, keeps giving me sausage sarnies, dripping with grease.'

'All I get is white sliced filled with cabbage leaves and dripping some kind of garlic laden oil, supposed to be good for me, low cholesterol or something, I tried feeding them to the pigeons at lunchtime, and   now they take off faster than a Boeing 747 soon as they see the bread bag.'

'Talking of food, I'm getting peckish, fancy a round of cheese and pickle, do you?'

'Yeah, go on then, I'll get them, want another pint, do you?'

'Cheers Dennis and a packet of pork scratchings and some pickled eggs would go down a treat.' At least if he had a mouthful of something, anything, he wouldn't have to make conversation.

'Lynda gone to bingo, has she?' he ventured when he could spin his snack out no longer.

'No, she's at her night class.'

'I wish my wife would do a night class, preferably an all-night class, if you know what I mean, Dennis.'

'Yes, I think Lynda would think that was good too.' Shit thought Fred, 'do you want another pint, or what?' Should I mention work thought Fred, quickly running out of ideas to pacify Dennis the Depressed? Probably not a good idea as he knew   Dennis when he had left school and started to work for the council as a painter

'I'm a council official,' he would always say, 'a white-collar job,' he would add, well it was in effect as he was Mr White Gloss Man. Within a year he'd been given an apprentice, Wayne, Mr Emulsion Man.

They'd been a team, together for years until last year when the council had sold them out to a housing association. Now Dennis and Wayne had lost their status and their white Bristol District Council van and had to drive around in what they considered to be a milk float, an ecologically acceptable vehicle, with a parpy little horn and no guts.

'Saw your Lynda the other day, she's changed Dennis.'

'And not for the better,' snapped Dennis. 'There was a time I was master in my own house, but she's taken to arguing with me, telling me what she wants to see on the telly, before I've even had my tea. And that's another thing; we hardly ever have chips. Since she's been talking to her old school friends and started work, she's a different person.'

'Some people might call you a lucky sod; I wish my wife would transform herself. She's got a cracking figure and her hair's nice and she polishes her nails too. And if my wife put on knickers like your Lynda, by god I'd be a happy man.'

'What THE HELL do you know about my wife's knickers?'

'Nothing mate, calm down,' said Fred sweating slightly now. 'Only what I've heard down the factory, you know how those girls natter. They were just saying as they'd been to one of those knicker parties and saying that your Lynda bought a thong thingy. I'd tried to get the wife to go along but she said no way was she missing a Coronation Street special.' As Dennis sipped his beer and idly watched Charlie Chivers empty the fruit machine of the very last ten pence by the look of it. Fred decided to call it a night.

'See you Dennis, chin up mate.'

SIXTEEN

Aries: A stranger shakes up your ideas and shows you that truth is stranger than fiction.

At six years I had written a rude word on the blackboard during break time, and the indomitable Miss Briffitt, clad in tweed skirt and wearing horn rimmed glasses had admonished me in front the whole class. As she had stripped me of my privileges, I had felt a warm trickle down my legs which was absorbed by my white ankle socks. I sobbed as I saw the yellowish tinge knowing that my Mum would be bound to ask what had happened. I had loved being milk monitor and while everyone else was outside skipping and playing marbles I'd been putting the straws in the third of a pint bottles warming nicely against the large radiator. But my solitude was, of course, what gave me away. That old familiar feeling was creeping back as I stood on teetering heels in front of Dennis, Ivy Gary, Mark, and Nita, and I pursed my lips together, swallowing hard. At least I had avoided one problem tonight, no socks and no knickers either come to that. For tonight I was going out with the girls- again. Hence the third degree.

'But why do you want to see a fortune teller?'

'Complete waste of time if you ask me,' sniffed Ivy.

'Well, I'm not asking you, it's a bit of fun, that's all, and she's a clairvoyant, not a fortune teller.'

'Same difference if you ask me.'

'Suppose she s s says something that you don't want to hear, what are you going to d-d-d-do then?'

'It's just a laugh; I'm not taking it seriously.'

'It's a lot of money for a laugh,' countered Dennis, 'and it's a load of old rubbish.'

'How do you know? You've never been have you?'

'No, and I wouldn't neither, cos it's dangerous meddling in the future.'

'Well it sounds fun to me,' interrupted Nita 'who's going, can I come too?'

'Yes, of course you can, there's me and Mandy, Lolly and Cilla. I was thrilled to think that my daughter in law actually wanted to come out with me. Usually I was deemed to be an authority on household purchases such as the purchase of a set of saucepans or similar, but never a soul mate, a comrade, a friend.

'We won't be late, I'll bring back chips if you like?' feeling, as always, this need to appease everyone. Dennis looked at me through narrowed eyes which seemed to pierce through my clothing. If anyone else had done that I'd have felt a surge of excitement, but with Dennis I just felt irritated. Why couldn't he jump up and ravish me, like any decent husband. Still, that would make me late, and I was going out whatever they said.

'Just wait while I do my lipstick and go to the loo and I'll be right there.' Nita broke the awkward moment. Gary glared at her departing back and father and son crossed their arms and legs simultaneously before glumly turning their attention to the telly. At least they could watch the gardening programme together and make lewd comments on the braless presenter in peace. Then they could immerse themselves in the football, clutching cans of beer and nibbling peanuts, many of which would invariably end up down the back of the sofa. A car pulled up and the honking of a pink Ford Escort, pink fluffy dice swinging from the mirror, filled the street. I hurriedly opened the door hoping to quieten them down but of course Mandy used this opportunity to shout our intentions to all the neighbours.

'Come on Lynda, we'll be late, and I'm dying to know who I'll be shagging next year.'

'Nita, hurry up,' I urged, scattering cushions everywhere in an attempt to find somewhere to sit. I was pulling my shirt down with one hand and the other was attempting to hide my cleavage.

'That Wonderbra has done the trick hasn't it?' remarked Cilla. 'You could smuggle an illegal immigrant through customs between your tits now.'

'You don't think I've overdone it do you?' I asked anxiously. 'I don't want to look like mutton dressed......'She screeched with laughter.

'With a body like yours they're not going to notice your face don't quite match until much, much later - just enjoy the moment.' She had this knack of making you feel brilliant before dropping you firmly back into place with a cruel but, as usual, accurate observation.

'Remember not to apply for the job of Agony Aunt, won't you?' I begged. She used to knock me sideways with her observations but now I could almost shrug them off.

'Anyway,' she continued, not flustered in the least, 'these young lads always fancy a woman with experience you know, my brother still leers at you and dribbles constantly when you are around.'

'Oh great, so I'm a magnet for pimply youths with fertile imaginations am I?'

'Yeah, they're fertile all right' she screeched, digging me hard in the ribs. And that Mr Manley fancies you.'

'But he goes on Saga holidays and gets excited about cheaper car insurance.'

'Gawd, you're so picky, aren't you?'

'I just want romance, nothing heavy, and someone my age-ish, unattached, rich, and handsome.'

'I should widen your choice, and your legs come to that,' noted Cilla, never lost for a retort. For one moment I desperately wanted to go back to my comfortable life, which fitted me like a favourite pair of slippers. What was I thinking of? Whatever I could achieve did not include shedding twenty years.

'Come on cheer up,' said Nita, 'We'll have time for a quick one after seeing this woman. Then you'll feel better, you've got a good life really. Better than my Mum anyway. My Dad wouldn't let her go out with the girls.'

'But your Mum wears a sari, doesn't work, and has six other children at home; she doesn't even speak much English, does she?'

'No, anyway, what do you think this witch will be like, I reckon she'll be called Lola, have a long flowing skirt, an aura of mysticism, and a crystal ball.'

'And smell of joss sticks too,' said Cilla, 'come on we're here. You jump out, I'll go and park.' Edna sat us down in her hall and one by one we were invited into the front room of her little semi. She left me till last. I looked around, surprised by the lack of spiritualism. Every available surface was filled with plastic flowers which blended into the huge patterned wallpaper depicting a cottage garden. The only item which attracted me was sat on the brown velvet tablecloth – a pack of cards. I sat opposite Edna squirming slightly as she peered at me through owl like eyes. She blinked, shaking her head, wiping her hands on her flowery pinny.

'I don't know what you were expecting my dear, but there is very little I am able tell you about your future, though I know a great deal about your past.'

'But!' I stuttered. That's it then I thought I've obviously had my life that was it, there's nothing else for me. I might as well give up now. I had listened enthusiastically as the girls before me had emerged laughing and giggling, telling me of their anticipated marriages, their children, their lovers and enemies. My hopes and dreams came crashing down along with a large vase of dusty chrysanthemums. Edna jumped up, and I perceived the accident as an omen.

'Oy,' she screamed at a disgruntled Siamese cat, 'get out of here. Sorry about that, my dear.'

'Shall I go now?' I stood up reluctantly, thrusting a couple of notes at her.

'No, sit down, I still have a lot to say, and I'll start but you must tell me when you don't want to hear any more. Your life is going to change, so much you can't imagine. But I can't reveal your future to you, because you're not ready for it. Not yet you aren't.' She had me hooked.

'Let's have a cuppa my dear.' As we sipped our tea, she told me of my past, Dennis was there, the stuttering man with a garden spade, and so was the oh so deaf one. She mentioned my two sons, who she saw playing in long grass, picking up worms. Edna didn't seem to know they were all grown up now. I emerged an hour later, much subdued. I wished I had taken a pen and paper to take notes, or recorded it, for she had not stopped talking all that time and I couldn't take it all in.

'Gawd, we thought you were never coming out, we nearly left you behind.'

'What did she tell you?'

'You got your money's worth, didn't you?'

'Going to run off with your lover, are you?'

'No, she's going to be rich and famous.' I shook my head, refusing to answer them. But one day they would find out, for Edna had told me- I had a future. I would get a life and it was just around the corner. Whether Dennis was going to be a part of it, she had said, was up to me.

'Come on,' I said, 'the drinks are on me.' We left the pub when the publican turned the lights out and pushed us out the door and I forgot the promised chips, but it didn't matter, because the house was quiet, they were both in bed. Dennis was snoring loudly and had left me a note. Thanks, it said, for nothing, I had to make my own supper, and there's no cheese left for my sandwiches. I punched the pillow and lay down heavily hoping to disturb him at least, but he didn't stir. Bearing in mind Edna's words I poked him in the back and felt relieved when he grunted.

SEVENTEEN

Aries: the same old, same old is not for you – anymore.

'I haven't seen you for ages,' shouted Karen from number 17. 'I suppose now that you're a working girl you've forgotten all your old friends?' she chided. She continued sweeping her path and our brushes met at the gutter.

'Do you know?' she started, eager to lean on her broom for a minute, 'I've always wished that you could pull up a bit of pavement and sweep the rubbish underneath. That's what I used to do indoors before we had fitted carpets you know. The rugs did get a bit lumpy after a while though,' she added thoughtfully. I grinned; I'd missed her. She was always cheerful and happy with her lot. Perhaps I should spend more time with her; work was definitely making me unsettled. I reminded her about our party.

'You're both coming round tonight aren't you, you haven't forgotten? I'm going to town to get all the food in.'

'How could I forget Lynda? It's as big a tradition as Christmas as far as the men are concerned so don't forget the crackers. It's only about six months to next Christmas so one of the shops will be bound to have them on the shelves now.' I shook my head, all this for the Eurovision Song Contest.

'Dennis is inside sharpening his pencils for the scoring and whistling past winners' songs.'

'You don't need to tell me, Dave stuck his head through the serving hatch this morning singing save all your kisses for me, before I'd had my first cup of tea, it was scary.'

'Still, it gives us a chance to natter over a glass of wine doesn't it?'

'Yes, interspersed with supplying cold beer and pickled onions and ignoring their extremely loud shushes of course.'

'I'm looking forward to your Dennis getting on his high horse and saying — It's not the same without Katie Boyle is it Dave?'

I laughed and assumed the pose and accent 'Norway nil points.' Quite honestly, I'd been dreading this evening but Karen as usual had reassured me. It had been a mistake telling the girls at work my plans for the weekend.

'You're barmy,' Mandy had giggled.

'Nobody watches that until they go into a rest home,' Polly had added. I'd squirmed as the rest of the department including the fearsome Miss Butterworth had a good laugh at my expense. Malcolm-in-despatch nice bum, sexy smile, splattered his coffee all down his brown overall.

'Now who's talking with their mouth full?' Cheryl had retorted.

'Yeah, well,' he muttered, as he wrung out the excess into the waste bin, 'we all know you're the expert at doing two or three things while your mouth is full don't we?'

Karen's' lilting tones brought me back to today, here and now.

'Watch out Lynda, that young postie's coming down the hill at breakneck speed again.' We leapt into the hedge, but he managed to pull up inches away from us by applying his size nines to the pavement.

'Haven't they given you new brakes yet?' enquired Karen. But as usual he just smiled, brilliant white teeth flashing like shooting stars from his ebony face. He handed me a pile of envelopes and then pulled one for Karen from his sack. We admired his sturdy legs pedalling off and stole a last lingering look at his post office issue shorts covering his generous bottom, overhanging the saddle.

'I'll never understand how he gets the post to the right house; he can't speak a word of English as far as I know.'

'When I was tiny,' reminisced Karen, 'I was given a dolly, black as coal it was, but when I undressed it the body was white. Do you know, I thought for more years than I care to mention that black people were only that colour on their limbs and faces.' I smiled as I shuffled through my post.

'Aah here's one from Julie, we can read it tonight during Sweden's entry. She writes a fantastic letter and obviously has an exciting life. She works in a massage parlour you know.

'Can't wait,' grinned Karen 'See you later.'

She brushed the final pile of rubbish into the gutter, neatly covering the single yellow lines outside her home. I added my contribution and went inside. Ivy would have fun this afternoon, sitting with her garibaldi and cuppa, watching the Tesco customers parking unwittingly, ever hopeful of seeing Tara-the-Terror

120

traffic warden doing her rounds. We squashed into the dark front room that night, soft lighting couldn't disguise the brown woodwork and flock wallpaper that had been so popular in the forties and, being sold off cheaply in the sixties, had been hung without consultation by Dennis. I absolutely hate those programmes on telly that do makeovers because I would have been entirely happy with most of them before the transformation. Dennis and Dave had grabbed the armchairs, balanced beers in one arm and a plate of nibbles on the other and were busy scoring. Spain, as usual, had entered the same song as they had entered in the previous ten years but the bit of fluff singing it had resorted this year to wearing a see through top. And it was a very bouncy song too. It got the boys vote anyhow. Me and Karen sat on the dining chairs and used the sideboard as our table. We tucked into huge fresh chocolate éclairs, eyes shut, dreaming our dreams, blissfully content for a couple of minutes and our moods softened. We then both read the letter from Julie. I don't know whether I can face you, it had started. I could hear her nasally tones even now, some twenty years on. My life has been rather a disaster. I married the wrong man, at the wrong time, and I wish I could start my life all over again. Now where have I heard that before? Then I married again, basically because I was pregnant. I had been an only child, which I had hated so, within six weeks of having our Craig I thought what the hell and got pregnant again. It seemed like a good idea at the time. My husband Jim is good with the kids, they look just like him, but it's no love affair. I work four nights a week at the 'health and fitness club', all above board. But I know, that if I had worked harder at school, had more chances, more help I could be doing the same job, but my job title would be Psychiatrist, earning a big fat salary instead of a poxy basic wage. When I read about all the others and their lives, well I worry that I'm going to look like a loser. Look at you Lynda, everything you've done? I felt a guilt trip looming, remembering my exaggerations, the bending of the truth, the omissions in my correspondence.

Anyway, it continued, I'm not ashamed of my family, but I would like you to see them before the day so it's not such a shock to you. I've posted a picture on the net, here's the web address. I could hardly wait to get to work, access the net, and see for myself. Was he an axe murderer, did he have two heads, were her kids gruesome? I just couldn't imagine. At least she was going to turn up, and bring them with her which was more than I was going to do. Dennis, I had told them, worked on the rigs! Karen and I enjoyed that evening and clapped when Ireland won again. And Dennis produced, from the sealed envelope he had lodged with his mother earlier that week, the winner he had predicted. He'd missed his vocation, that man, now why couldn't he do that with the lottery numbers!

'Ring me,' said Karen, 'as soon as you've got to work and seen what she wants to hide. I need to know.'

'Me too,' I replied. Perhaps everyone has secrets I thought. Still haven't been abroad, must look into that. I made a mental note -Travel agents after work on Monday.

EIGHTEEN

Aries: Venus is lighting a fire – don't stand too close!

I woke to find the sun shining, the sparrows gossiping on the window ledge and a greasy indent on the pink frilly pillow beside me. I must, despite my firm belief that I had been awake all night, have dropped off. Dennis had gone to work, leaving only the lingering odour of discount after-shave.   I could hear Ivy crashing around in the kitchen; god knows how we had any plates left. The kitten, Des, short for despair, joined me; assured by my reluctance to get up that it must be Sunday morning. As the clock was not yet bullying me to rise, I caressed him gently, enjoying his contented purr. He stretched out as my strokes got longer and bolder, fur electrified, and claws extending and retracting in a frenzy of excitement. I was green with envy — that should be me, with a heaving, grunting insatiable husband on top of me fulfilling my every desire, leaving me begging for more. Dennis had other ideas of course. Once a week after Match of the day. (Not applicable if he was on Sunday morning overtime). Saturday evening was rather like reading a beloved fairy tale, well-thumbed and predictable. He would appear wearing only the bottom half of striped pyjamas with more black holes than Cheddar caves fastened by what once must have been white length of knotted cord. That and the lick of toothpaste clinging onto his bottom lip gave me that happy ever after sign.

It wasn't bad just tame, repetitive, but it was one step up from tackling the ironing.

'You should count yourself lucky,' Karen had retorted unsympathetically during one of our girly chats 'my husband keeps his socks on, takes his teeth out and shouts 'tonight's the night if you play your cards right.' Perhaps I would come back in my next life as a cat, I considered. Although I was looking forward to work today and the chance for a sneak preview of Julie's possibly bizarre family, the day was overshadowed by the news whispered to me by my tearful daughter in law Nita. Last night she had confided that she thought she might be pregnant. She had sworn me to secrecy, even from her husband, my son. I could sympathize with her for she was only twenty-one, not even started her life yet. But what would my son think? I rather thought he'd be happy, for it wouldn't change his life too much would it? My lack of enthusiasm had only served to depress her further.

'Boots, tomorrow, testing kit,' I had whispered with her goodnight hug, 'ring me, if you want to.' I sat up, stared in the dressing table mirror, and saw an imminent grandmother, a middle-aged woman going through the change, and not the thirty something I had been trying to become for the last six months. Wasn't it odd? We were now united - the two of us desperately wanting what we had always called the curse, to come and put our lives back in order. I jumped up and poor Des had to cling for dear life on to the candlewick bedspread. If we'd had a duvet like everyone else he'd have been half way down the hall by now.

'I'm sorry Des, I didn't mean it,' and I grabbed him, held him tight, stroking him vigorously waiting for him to calm down. By the time we'd reached the bathroom he had forgiven me and was purring again.

'Shit, I've put on two and a half pounds,' I screeched before realizing that Des was a sleeping partner in this unexpected weight gain. I dropped him into the linen basket where he curled up immediately. He particularly enjoyed sleeping nose deep into soiled underwear. Reincarnation as a cat was losing its appeal.

'Hell, I've still put nearly two pounds this week.' As I stood, willing the scales to recalibrate and purge the unwanted excess, a crashing sound from the kitchen filled the tiny terraced house.

'Bugger,' I heard 'Bugger, bugger, bugger.' Monday morning! The twin bells of the clock shrilled in unison and it danced off the table, clanging onto the floor. After twenty years, today of all days it had decided to shuffle over to the wrong edge and instead of hitting the rug it hit the floorboard and the glass shattered. What a day, and it was only seven thirty.

'Shit.' I faced the moaner from hell, who had only burnt the toast and escaped as quickly as possible.

By coffee break, I was feeling better, normality prevailed and as I nibbled my Kit Kat, I enjoyed the chatter of the girls and their weekend adventures.

'Five Bacardi's he bought me, and he had his own condoms!' boasted Lolly.

'What about his mate, Byron wasn't it? Did you cop off with him then?' asked Polly who today had vivid purple streaks in her hair with matching eye shadow and had spent the first 'working' half hour pasting her new image from her mobile to the computer as a screen saver. She was now sending it through to dispatch so they could all enjoy it too!

'Yeah, he was OK but all he talked about was his ex-girlfriend, even when we were doing it.'

'What, he compared you like did he?'

'No, he just called me Angie a couple of times, but he was very drunk.'

'Surprised he kept in up then,' sniffed Mandy. 'Well, he did, cos I offered him something very special,'

'Yeah, what was that then?' She poked her tongue out, displaying three glittering studs. 'Had them done Saturday, down the precinct, buy two get one free. It's like giving them an electric shock with this - works every time.' I kept typing, but my concentration was minimal I realized as I saw the quote listing sidebeard, four dipping chairs, two cavers, all with our traditional solid pork legs. I pressed the spell check quickly.

'So how was your Saturday night then Lynda, all sex and debauchery?'

'Oh, sorry I forgot- you had Terry Wogan to give you the ultimate orgasm added to the supreme thrill of seeing Norway go home with fuck all again.'

'Actually, I had a great time; we had a few drinks and a lovely girlie evening in. We don't all have to sleep around and drink to excess to enjoy ourselves you know.'

'Soooorry forgot for a moment you were well on the way to becoming a golden oldie.'

'Haven't you got any work to do?' I countered - I felt queasy, I wondered if I was beginning the countdown to becoming a grandmother. Should I ring Nita and see if she'd got her kit? No, I didn't really want to know, not yet, not until I had to. For once I was glad to see Miss. Butterworth the supervisor waddling down. It was lunchtime when I was able to contact Nita. We whispered to each other, difficult when you are on the phone and very irritating.

'Did you go?'

'Yes,' Nita hissed.

'Did it work?'

'No.'

'Oh dear.'

'No, it's OK.'

'You mean you're happy, it's what you want?'

'Well I don't know if it is or not, I can't, at the moment, if you know what I mean.' I was getting very confused now, muttering 'Yes, I do, well no I don't really.' Exasperated now, I was relieved when Nita said 'Can I come over to see you tonight?'

'Yes, of course.'

'Will you be able to talk?'

'Yes,' I hesitated 'and no. Ivy is going to Bingo, but Dennis is around.'

'Right, well I'll bring Gary and we'll send them up the pub.' Her voice suddenly became shrill. 'It's O.K my end now, everyone else has gone out. Could you do the test for me?' I was totally baffled now

'But I thought you had, and you were?'

'No, I've just got the kit.'

'I fail to see how me doing the test will tell me whether you're p…….' Mandy had casually moved close to me and although she appeared distracted adjusting the straps on her new 40 DD bra her breath was shallow as she eavesdropped. I changed the receiver to my other ear.

'No, I'll provide the sample but you test it for me, I just haven't got the nerve.'

'I see, OK yes, no problem. So, you haven't — you know.'

'No, and I'm so worried,' her voice suddenly penetrating, 'I think I may have left the cooker on.'

'Pardon?'

'Hello Alison, I'm just saying hello to Alison who's just come in to ask me out to lunch.'

'Right - I'll see you later then.'

'OK, see you tonight.' I replaced the receiver. I would just have to wait.

'Was that Nita?' asked Mandy, still trying to manoeuvre her breasts into a bra cup clearly two sizes too small. Is she OK?'

'Yes, she's fine.'

'So why did she screech like that?'

'Oh, she remembered she'd left something in the oven I think.'

'Do you think this fits me OK?' She lifted her jumper and I was confronted with two footballs trying to wriggle out of what looked like a luminous blue string bag.

'It depends if you're going for comfort or looks I suppose.'

'What do you think?' she giggled; causing a significant rippling effect that made Malcolm-from-dispatch, who had just appeared in the doorway, to drop his tray of notes. They fluttered to the floor and he

128

absentmindedly tried to scoop them up but his eyes remained firmly affixed on Mandy's chest. Mandy being Mandy was in no hurry to pull down her jumper. Without warning she jumped forward growling menacingly causing Malcolm's head to collide with the corner of a desk. He groaned and collapsed. Mandy took this opportunity to step right over him and gaze down over his recumbent body.

'Oh Malcolm, now you can tell all your mates you've been between my legs can't you?' she drawled. With a wiggle and a high knee lift she then left only pausing to shout, 'see you Lynda; I'll be late back, cover for me.' Malcolm took my proffered glass of spring water with shaking hands, and then scampered off and, with the office to myself; I dived onto the Internet to see if I could solve the mystery of Julie's family. Her blog sounds just ordinary – I could picture her now, blond with the faintest hint of ginger, fair to the point of her skin seeming almost translucent. What I didn't expect to see however, when I opened her photos was her cuddling two of the blackest, most gorgeous children with ebony eyes. Beside them was the Incredible Hulk, the Jamaican version, wow. I would write to her when I had a minute, what had she been trying to tell me - but failed? If I had a hunk of a husband like that and smiling picture book children I would be telling the world. I was still puzzling when I was washing up in the evening. I'd spent ten minutes finding Ivy's lucky hat in an effort to get her out the door and had one eye on Dennis, who looked as if he would be asleep before Nita and Gary arrived. I'd hidden his slippers and spilt tea over his rag of a newspaper to ensure that he had no reason to decline a night in the pub with his son. By promising them a late supper Nita and I were able to shoo them out to the Butchers Arms.

'Come on then, get it out, we'll do it now.' Nita, tears looming, handed me a brown paper bag.

'Perhaps we should wait a while, I'm only a couple of weeks late, and I may have got the dates wrong anyway. And.....'

'No Nita, the sooner you know, the sooner you can make your choice.'

'But I don't really have a choice do I, I'm married.'

'Let's just do the test shall we, we can argue about the pros and cons afterwards. Besides it may be negative and we can just sit and get drunk.' I unwrapped the shiny package with some difficulty and unfolded the instructions.

'Here you go, go on do it now.'

'But I don't want a wee at the moment, let's have a drink first.'

'No Nita, just go and squeeze - a tiny drop, that all it takes.' In the end we watched two soaps and three quarters of a programme about football heroes of the fifties and sixties   before I could persuade her to go to the bathroom. She returned within minutes and slid into Dennis's armchair, curled into a ball and drained a full glass of white wine. I stared avidly at the screen and the scenes of Kruger National Park.

'And the pregnancy of an elephant lasts for sixteen months,' boasted David Attenborough before I could punch the remote-control button.

'Cooee,' echoed through the hall and Ivy tottered in clutching a six-foot-high pink Bertie Bassett. 'I won, now all I need is a grandchild to give this to.'

'I'm going to take out my contact lens,' explained Nita, dashing past Ivy, 'my eyes are so sore, I'll be right back.'

NINETEEN

Scorpio: A twinkle in the eye could trigger a dilemma for all the family.

'Ivy - I'll just check on Nita, then I'll make us all a nice cup of tea,' I shouted as I darted up the narrow stairs. I found Nita crouched on the cold mottled green lino floor, her mouth stuffed with what Dennis called his flannel but I knew better as his multipurpose cloth. Although it was obviously placed there to subdue the sobs which racked her body, I knew I had to relieve her of it immediately before she succumbed to rabies, mad cow disease and whatever other germs were held in that dank infested towelling square. I heaved as I touched it — normally I would only risk contact through pink rubber gloves and a long pair of wooden tongs, but this was an emergency. Trivial words, frivolous sayings spewed out of my mouth.

'It's not the end of the world, Nita. Once you feel that little person inside you, you'll feel differently' and the more she bawled the more proverbs hovered waiting to gush out.

'You're shutting the stable door after.........and don't drink that water!' I yelled as she grasped the bathroom mug, unaware that Ivy's spare set of National Health teeth were lurking inside presumably conducting trials on a brand-new range of antibiotics. Inside I was howling too, my stomach churned, though mainly through guilt. She would get over the shock - I knew that. Gary would be over the moon, she would give up work, they might even move out from her parents' house and get a little place of their own and she could become little Miss Housewife-and-mother and probably be very happy for a while. I, however, would become a white-haired grandmother, with shadowed top lip, plump thighs, bulging stomach with copious babysitting responsibilities. And worse still - here I was thinking, once again, of me, me, me.

'Now Nita, pack it in or the oh so deaf one will hear you. Wipe those tears away and we'll have a garibaldi with our cup of tea.' Cheers for the great British cure all. I lay in bed that night; Dennis snoring gently beside me re-reading a letter that had come from another of the girls this morning. Time was ticking away and I still had not completed all those tasks I had set myself in order to hold my head up high at this damn reunion. Mother in law was still padding about and, unbeknown to me, had discovered, following a surreptitious inspection of the bathroom waste bin, a small folded sheet of paper giving detailed instructions on the significance of the thin blue line. Two and two make five to a dotty old woman! My mind however, is on the six-page letter from Madeleine who used to be able to spin a hoop around her waist for the entire lunchtime without a break, whilst eating an apple and relating classified details of the sex lives of our teachers. I have never thought until today just how she knew all these sordid little facts. She always wore tight fitted blue knickers from Marks and Sparks whilst I had the school shop issue, baggy with a pocket for a hanky. Just thinking about her made my nostrils flare. I wonder what she has become. I secretly hoped that she had seven children, with seven anonymous fathers. A husband in prison on a ten stretch, and was suffering from alopecia, thread veins and irritable bowel syndrome - none of which was probable, for she had enclosed a photo. She was on board what looked to me like a jet-setters yacht. She was small boned, fragile looking with long blonde highlighted hair and wore a Barbie doll sized bikini. I peered hoping to discover flaws, but no - she still looked about twenty-five but it was definitely her. I'd recognize that supercilious smile anywhere. She was being groped by a gorgeous tanned Walt Disney type pirate. I glanced down at my buccaneer.

'Is it time to get up?' snorted Dennis, raising his greasy head from the pillow.

'No, go back to sleep Dennis.'

'And I've run out of s-socks again, it's only since you started work...'

'Dennis it's nearly midnight, just wear yesterdays, they'll match your week-old underpants,' I added in a whisper, carefully placing a pillow over his head so he could sleep undisturbed. Moments or perhaps minutes later his feet twitched so I lifted my hands releasing the pressure. His snorting resumed immediately.

And that's another thing that annoyed me; I still had a twin tub washing machine. No amount of hinting would persuade Dennis that I needed an automatic. Sleep rage kicked in. If it was good enough for his mother it was good enough for me. The girls at work collapsed with laughter when they found out and I endured many endless sniggers and sly remarks about the adaptability of this unit and how they wished they had one. After all I must be saving myself a fortune on batteries. Mandy had heard that Anne Summers was thinking of selling them in her autumn range! Yes, I admit it did have its uses, but lust and naked desire fly out the window when the reek of boiling hankies fill the back kitchen and I was seldom alone in my own house to enjoy the experience anyway.

TWENTY

Pisces: Beware of meddling in other people's affairs!

The disembodied voice of the oh so deaf one echoed from the bedroom. Foreplay is she saying foreplay? Did I hear her right? - has she gone totally round the bend? Reluctantly I put my head round the door.

'Could you buy me some four-ply when you're out Lynda, I'll pay you back when I collect my pension.'

'Oh yes - of course,' I agreed immediately, 'um, what colour?'

'Oh, yellow I think, that's neutral isn't it?'

'You haven't knitted for ages, what are you going to make?' Her teeth, unused to accommodating a smile, jumped out onto her lap, clattering against her steel knitting needles.

'Oh, just a little something, I don't know yet really, but my fingers are stiffening up, I thought I might help my Arthur Itis.'

'Arthur, that reminds me Ivy, Arthur Doveton died this week.'

'Yes, Margaret phoned, I'm going to the funeral on Wednesday. Still when one door closes another door opens - that's what they say,' she added mysteriously. I returned her smile but was puzzled. I'd thought she was quite fond of him. What was she twittering about now? Maybe I should book her in at the doctors; perhaps she needs her medication adjusting?

'Terrible, he was in my class at infants you know. I knew his feet would kill him down in the end.'

'His feet?' I queried, 'he died of a heart attack.'

'Yes,' she replied smugly 'but he was on his way to the chiropodist.' I realized that I would never understand her I shook my head.

'I'll see you later.'

'Don't forget my wool.' Ivy ordered.

As usual I pulled the door shut by the letterbox and as usual it came off in my hand. I dumped it on top the milk crate, where it would stay until Dennis pushed it back on with his boot when he came home from work. I can't imagine Verity Osbourne-Box in her rose covered cottage putting up with that- I bet she's got a little handyman. And come to that she's probably got a woman that does too. My nail varnish was chipped again. I don't know why I bothered. My good mood was diminishing fast. Think positively I told myself. Damn, I suddenly remembered. Nita's test was positive; my heart sank as I saw myself holding a snotty baby. God I could feel my shoulders getting rounder already. Those pregnancy tests I wondered, did they turn blue if it was a boy and pink if it was a girl? I must ask. Thinking skeins of wool made me cogitate - it flashed across my mind that Ivy might have inkling that Nita was pregnant — had she been listening at keyholes again? I was shocked to find myself at the factory already. It was a wonder I didn't get knocked down walking along in a daydream all the time. Pull yourself together Lynda. One look at Lorraine's tearstained face brought me back to reality, she charged at me like a bull knocking me sideways and sobbed into my shoulder.

'Whatever's the matter, come on tell me?' More sobs.

'Is it a man?' (It had to be a man.) She bawled. I stroked her hair away from her face and handed her a tissue from my handbag. It still held everything I might need for a fortnight in Blackpool, despite my attempts at minimalism.

'I wish you were my Mum,' she whimpered. I bit my lip, gritted my teeth and tried very hard to retain the agony aunt pose.

'Come on; tell me, I can possibly help- it's probably not that bad – it's probably something I've done a hundred times.'

'Oh, I don't think so,' was the blunt reply. Her crying turned into a snivel as Miss Butterworth swept into the room. She tossed big brown files into the already overfilled in trays then rooted herself firmly in the centre of the room, arms crossed.

'We've some big orders come in; I want you all to work hard. I expect all these orders to be processed today, even if you have to work through lunch. That'll make a change for some of you of course; you're not even used to working through the morning. Lorraine, blow your nose and get to work. Polly, four -inch long fingernails nails are not practical for a touch typist- take them off now. And Mrs. Fisher - please ensure that the internet is disconnected for the whole of the morning with the exception of your desk. I'm sure you can be trusted not to dally in these chit-chat rooms.'

'Yes Miss Butterworth,' we chorused.

'I'll be back at 4.45.' The door hissed shut - her heels clicked swiftly up the corridor. We all held our

138

breath as the clicks got louder again. Her head bobbed around the door.

'And Cilla?'

'Yes, Miss Butterworth?'

'Do not go into dispatch today unless you put a cardigan on - old Tom is still waiting for his pacemaker.'

'Yes, Miss Butterworth.' When the coast was clear I hissed across the room.

'Lorraine?'

'It's nothing Lynda; I'll catch you later.' I missed the wool shop as I stayed late to finish the orders - the girls had one excuse after another and obviously prior commitments like dates came first. But I was home by six thirty ready to invade the freezer on the lookout for ready meals. Dennis jumped out from behind the kitchen door, the table was laid and Ivy was sat waiting, knife and fork in hand.

'I'm sorry, Ivy - I couldn't get to the shop for your wool today.'

'Never mind; tomorrow will do. I might even take a walk down there myself.'

'Tea's ready,' chirruped Dennis, 'come and sit down' he added, patting the chair, 'one of my specials. Just whipped it up when I realized you were going to be late.' I struggled to keep my eyes from popping out of their sockets and my chin from hitting my chest. Des seized his chance and crept onto my lap, purring loudly. They were both beaming at me and when Dennis produced, like a magician, a bunch of chrysanthemums I wondered what they had to tell me. Had I won the lottery? Or maybe Dennis had been made redundant. No, there had to be something more.

'I said Lynda, how many fish fingers do you want?'

'Um, two please, Dennis' I stared down at my plate as he plonked four down beside the peas.

'Got to keep your strength up!'

'You have dear; you're looking quite peaky,' added Ivy, 'Put your feet up after tea, I'll do the dishes.'

My phone then flashed - you have a new text message. False alarm, going to the pub, sorted. Cheers see you tomorrow. Lolly xxx. Someone had got their life back in order then, fantastic, just wish it was me.

TWENTY- ONE

Aries: In a dreamy sort of week it may be hard to keep your feet on the ground.

I made my excuses, 'just going down the greenhouse Ivy, to water the tomatoes, won't be long,' I called as I fled out the back.

'Don't lift anything heavy then,' came the response from the oh so deaf one.

'No, I won't,' I replied, inwardly picturing the large club hammer which I was going to bring down on her, half price for pensioners blue rinse hair, if she persisted in her conviction that I was pregnant. I'd put them both in the picture, several times. But she was still clicking away in buttercup yellow and Dennis persisted in winking at me, playfully patting his middle aged spread every time he saw me. I phoned Nita from my newly acquired mobile. It played fifty different melodies, a neat game of blackjack, but had proved very reticent about actually dialling my contacts. However, I had a terrific signal from the garden and peace and privacy down there too. I'd received several text messages from school friends and hoped that I would soon be able to reply without needing the manual and a magnifying glass.

'Nita, it's me - have you told Gary yet?'

'I can't because we're not talking at the moment; he's being very difficult.'

'Then text him, email him, put an advert in the paper, I don't care, but he has to know. What do you mean he's being difficult?'

'I'm just so tired all the time, and I throw up every time I smell beer, which is every night this week because Gary keeps going to the pub with his Dad, and I keep crying, I can't help it, and Gary just shouts at me.'

'That's because he can't understand why you're like this. You're pregnant Nita - and if he knew he was going to be a Dad he'd be over the moon, and then he'd tell me and then I could tell him how you feel and then he would be nice to you.'

'But he should have guessed I'm pregnant,' she replied stubbornly.

'No Nita,' I sighed 'he's a man — he needs to be told. And then he'll say how did that happen? But after that he'll come to terms with it and you'll soon see his little chest puff out as he tells all his mates what a clever boy he's been.' I attempted multi-tasking and turned on the hose, grabbing the loose end just as it started to weave wildly. Des suddenly shot out from underneath the staging where he had been sunbathing and I watched him chasing down the garden as if a Rottweiler   had him on the starter's menu. I looked down to see Dennis's tomato plants being swept away in a tidal wave, dropped the hose and quickly stemmed the flow breaking a precious nail on the tap.

'Bugger Nita I'll call you back, I'm having a crisis. Oh, and tell him tonight, no excuses.' I spent the next half hour replanting wilting plants back into the grow bags and asking them nicely to perk up before Dennis found them. I coaxed, cajoled and caressed but they showed limp indifference to my request, collapsing completely when I withdrew my hand. I remembered then that I had to remind Dennis to make an appointment with the doctor. But was the problem his or mine? Or both of ours? Was my becoming more of a woman making him less of a man? In spite of everything I still cared deeply for him, we'd stayed together for twenty-five years and I wasn't planning on changing my life that much. We'd had some good times. It all came flooding back to me - telling Dennis that he was going to be a father all those years ago. He'd strutted around for days telling everyone that he was going to be a d-d-d-d-dad. And it was d-d-due in d-d-d-December. We scoured the baby books, avoiding the section on d-d-d-delivery and decided not to call our son or daughter Donna, David or Darren. I'd loved him then and we had shared so many laughs, and even sharing the house with Ivy, recently widowed was not a problem. After all lots of young couples start out with their in-laws until they can get a place of their own don't they? She helped with my pregnancy, then lent a hand with the baby, and then stayed on whilst my second son arrived within the year. It wasn't until they both went to school that I noticed my anticipated independence had not arrived. My resident babysitter needed a babysitter herself. And now I was going to become a babysitter for my grandchild too. I crouched in the corner against a large bag of compost warmed by the sun, grabbed a soggy bundle of cat and cried. Des purred and snuggled in and within minutes we were both asleep.

TWENTY- TWO

Aries: With both Mars and Uranus vying for attention things could become a little confusing.

The persistent peeping of the smoke alarm lured me from my retreat where I had been giving the green tomatoes a good talking to whilst watering. Dennis stood on the narrow path outside the back door wearing a frilly pinny, wiping his forehead ferociously with a corner of the tea towel, frantically gesticulating with a spatula, announcing that tea was ready.

'I guessed that by the smoke billowing from the kitchen window,' I scolded gently. He cooked most nights now, fish fingers, sausages, frozen chips and waffles were his specialties and the nauseous smell of fried charred food was helping my diet considerably. As I had not yet convinced Dennis that I was not about to make him a proud Dad again he readily accepted that I wanted healthy alternatives and I was able to nibble on fresh salad whilst they tucked into transport cafe portions with eggs sunny side up.

'My gums have shrunk,' complained Ivy as her teeth plopped onto her plate landing neatly on top of a waffle scattering baked beans.

'Can you take me back to the dentist Lynda?' I sighed; I didn't really want to take time off work at the moment but as Dennis's job as a painter for the local housing association was under review I agreed. Two buses and a steep hill trailing a lumbering three toed sloth on a walking frame was not my idea of fun.

Please god she doesn't spit her teeth out on the bus. If only I had told Dennis I had passed my test I could have borrowed the car. I wanted to come clean. Should I get insurance first and leave it lying where he could see it or just go and pick him up from his next bowls match as a surprise? I mulled over the options as we ate.

'F-F-F-phone Lynda.'

'Oh right,' I jumped up, suddenly I could hear it tinkling away. Ivy and Dennis were looking at each other shaking their heads, and Ivy nodded knowingly, so she thought.

'Hello Lynda speaking,'

'Hi it's me, can you talk?'

'No - not really Nita, how about meeting up for lunch tomorrow?' I still got a quiver of excitement when arranging lunchtimes with the girls. I felt footloose and fancy free as Ivy would say, although she always sniffed and wrinkled her nose as she said it.

'Can you phone me from your mobile?'

'Sure, I'm just popping down to see if those cucumbers have shot up another inch again. Speak to you later.' Dennis was thrilled at my enjoyment of what had formerly been his hobby and was eager to share his knowledge with me. We now spent hours scrutinizing seed catalogues and he seemed much happier, more contented than in recent months. Our lovemaking had perked up and sometimes even on a Wednesday I would go to work with a smile and a kangaroo hop. Even Ivy seemed eager to please and we hadn't heard the 'it was good enough for your father' when shown the catalogues on new bathroom suites and not even a

'They only used to put white in public baths,' with that customary sniff of disapproval. Although I had suffered the whole week listening to the history of her one and only pregnancy.

'Tried it once didn't like it,' was her motto. No wonder then that Dennis was an only child and her late husband had suffered from terminal gloominess. But now I was feeling for poor Dennis. There were murmurings that redundancies were in the offing and his age was against him he said.

'These young lads coming in,' he complained 'they're not serving apprenticeships but are straight onto paint rollers, colour washes and even artexing ceilings.'

Dennis was affectionately known as white gloss man for that was his sole occupation and had been since he'd joined the council straight from school. Then the council subcontracted the work out and he was transferred to the association. And that, according to the gospel of St Dennis had been when the trouble started. They had wanted an all-rounder they said and a team player whatever that was.

'I'm a gloss man,' he had explained, and the bosses had sat back in their big fat director's chairs jingling the change in their pockets oozing disapproval.

'I don't do ceilings,' protested Dennis firmly. 'It gives me earache.' Having fallen out with them so soon he felt his time was nearly up and his heart wasn't in it anymore.

'I'll lose the company vehicle,' he whimpered. I shrugged - I had never been keen to travel in the battered panel van surrounded by paint pots, ladders and oily rags. But to Dennis it was status, and our little run around was for high days and holidays. He had now settled into the chair leaving the pans neatly stacked for me to do later.

'You read your paper Dennis; I'll check the greenhouse.' Eager to distract him I added, 'Have you ever thought about growing artichokes? Why don't you look it up while I'm watering?'

'We want things we can eat not stuff for flower arranging, you'll have me wearing green wellies if I'm not careful,' he chuckled.

'Yes,' I replied with a grin, and as old Mrs. Guthrie can't climb up to see over the wall anymore that's all you'll be wearing in the garden from now on.'

'Lynda, steady on Mother will hear.'

'No, she won't cos she's filled her ears with marshmallows again under that knitted tea cosy.'

'Oh mum,' hollered Dennis 'I'll get your hat for you, and some cotton wool.' I made my escape and Des joined me weaving in and out my legs as I made my way to the green retreat. I pulled the phone from my pocket.

'Hi, it's me, have you told him?'

'No,' she sobbed 'and the doctor wants me to go to the hospital for a scan, he said there's nothing wrong - it's just a precaution. But they always say that don't they.'

'No, not at all,' I tried to reassure her, 'I'm sure it's routine now, perhaps they think its twins or something.' She howled louder still.

'But I'll have to tell Garry, then won't I? He's going to notice two cots in the spare bedroom cos the door won't shut properly will it?'

'Nita' I intervened softly, 'He will notice before that you know, even before the Babygro's are fluttering on the line. He may take after his father but you won't keep it a secret much longer. Why don't you tell him and then he can take you to the hospital and be a part of it all?'

'No, I'm not telling him 'til I'm sure I can handle it, I want you to come with me please.'

'I'll pick you up,' I said proudly. It was my first journey without dual controls and a huffing puffing instructor and it left me dangerously wobbly. Nita grabbed my arm guiding me into ante natal where I collapsed into the chair.

'What name is it?' asked a kindly voice.

'Fisher,' Nita and I echoed

'Right, well I'll try to get you seen straight away, have you remembered to drink a pint of water?' I shook my head, water! I could down a double gin right now.

'Mrs. Fisher,' the nasally voice on the tannoy crackled. Room eight please. We both got up and shuffled, arm and arm, down the corridor. The jolly auxiliary scurried up to us, handing me a large squishy cup of water.

'Sorry it's probably a bit warm, but please drink it all.'

'You have it Nita — I'm not thirsty.'

'I think it was probably for me anyway,' Nita whispered. 'Unless you want to have a scan instead.' Most of the water managed to stay in the cup as I rushed to pass it over. My mind started to focus on the present as the curse of roundabouts, one-way roads and suicidal lollipop men faded.

'Oh Nita, I'm sorry. Come on drink up.' We peered at the screen and when we spotted that tiny curled up little foetus, we both cried.

'It's a baby- there Nita, can you see it, and it's got arms and legs and everything.'

'It's true,' she murmured, 'I'm going to have a baby; oh, I wish Gary was here.' We hugged and cried some more.

'I am so pleased for you Nita and for Gary. I can't wait to tell everyone at the office. Can you see if it's a boy or a girl?' I peered hard at the screen, but the view was similar to peering out through a giant car wash. I gave up trying and just hugged Nita.

'It's awesome,' we agreed. We enjoyed a cup of tea and a large slice of W.V.S ginger cake in the snack bar afterwards. Nita was debating various ways of telling Gary from arranging a quiet candle-lit meal for two but setting the table for three, to telling the nation by having it announced at half time at the football match, with the written confirmation on the score board. I couldn't remember telling Dennis at all when I was pregnant, but mulling it over, I expect his mother told him. Nita was happy to maintain a one-sided conversation all the way to the car whilst I dropped back into the memory bank. I realized that I could remember very little of the boy's early days. They were very close together and my parenting skills had been subject to close scrutiny, that I did remember, by the oh so deaf one. She had discouraged breast feeding, disposable nappies and dummies. I wish now I had followed my instincts, I vowed not to make this mistake with my daughter in law. I would be the perfect granny. Oh my god, what am I saying. My resolve has sailed away and I'm prepared to slip into wrinkles and tweed skirts. I checked the driving mirror. No, no, no. I won't let it happen. I sat up straight, thrust my boobs upwards and sucked in my tummy. I blew a kiss at the parking attendant and slipped into first gear.

TWENTY- THREE

*Aries: Combine your dreams with your instincts –
there's an enchanting world out there.*

'Lynda, what the hell have you got in there?'
gasped Polly as she passed me my handbag. 'It's bigger
than the bag I take to the Costa del Sol for a fortnight.'

'That doesn't surprise me,' said Mandy, joining in
one our coffee break chit chat sessions, which started
way before the trolley arrived. 'You only pack a thong
and an economy sized packet of strawberry flavoured
condoms.'

'Morning ladies,' bawled multi semi-skilled
Malcolm, whose duties in dispatch alternated between
dispensing coffee and biscuits in the morning, the chip
shop run at lunchtime and the tea urn and cakes at
three. At other times, as duty manager of the
washroom, he could be seen flourishing a toilet brush
and a wide variety of cleaning materials along with a
packet of fags and a lads mag tucked into his
waistband. His wet floor notice appeared with
monotonous regularity.

'Orders now being taken for cream cakes, pastries
and remember the special offer on jam doughnuts, one
pound on your arse with every three you put in your
belly.' He dropped onto one knee by my desk and laid
his head on my lap.

'Ask and it shall be yours — you delectable,
desirable, dishy woman.'

151

'Just coffee please Malcolm,' I replied returning his wicked smile. I patted his sloping shoulder but thought better of stroking his spotty face - though it was clearly scrubbed and the lingering odour of antiseptic advertised its ongoing treatment.

'Come on you pervert. Your coffee's getting cold,' complained Mandy. 'And how come you never offer me all those little extras?'

'Here's your coffee and biscuits,' he said avoiding a reply but adding, with an oversized wink at me, 'my scrubbing brush had taken quite a pounding recently, I'll have to put in a requisition form for a new one.' I moved my handbag to make way for the steaming mug. Yes, she was right, my handbag was heavy, but then, it concealed so many of my secrets. The lining held a driving license, a pregnancy test kit, bought for Nita as a spare in case she didn't believe the results of the first one amongst other things. And now, oh bliss, my virgin passport. Arriving today, it had barely landed on the doormat before being transferred into my bag and I was now free to respond to another glaring shortcoming. I could go abroad. The only trouble was that I had no idea where I could go, who I could go with and how to explain my absence from home. As usual I turned for advice from my friends, waving my passport in the air.

'Hey everyone, where would you suggest for a weekend away?' The response was unconstructive, unhelpful, and downright depressing.

'Germany is full of miserable gits,' noted Polly.

'France is OK, it's not too far away, it's quite pretty, but the food is naff, and it's full of French people.' said Lolly.

'But on the other hand, those French guys accents are knicker dropping in the extreme. Eyaw, eyaw, eyaw.'

'I wouldn't go to Italy again, my bum got so bruised, and they pinch anything that wobbles there,' reported a disembodied voice from the photocopier room. And they went on, and on. I nibbled my ginger nut wondering what was left to explore that wasn't war torn, ravaged by floods or inhabited by cannibals. Polly popped up with 'my mum and her fella went to the Isle of Man last year and they said that was brill.'

'That's not abroad though is it?' giggled Mandy.

'No, I know that' retorted Polly. 'But they have Bingo and ballroom dancing and all those things that Lynda would like — at her age,' she tailed off, seeing my eyes narrowing.

'Cheers Polly, you're right of course I should be looking at a Saga holiday rather than an exotic adventure.'

'That's it,' shrieked Lorraine, 'Come with us to France, me and her and her and unfortunately her.' She pointed at various smiling faces around the room 'And Malc, we're going on a coach trip. Off on Saturday morning at 5.30, spend the morning in the hypermarkets getting cheap plonk and sexy perfume and then spend the afternoon and evening in the bars chatting up the talent. Then back on the coach to sleep it off.'

'That sounds great – for a first trip,' I exclaimed 'but what do I tell Dennis?'

'You could tell him to truth.'

'No, he doesn't like foreigners, and he doesn't know I've got a passport anyway.'

'Right, well we'll think of something, come on let's phone up and book a place for you.' My brain was in overdrive for the rest of the morning thinking of explanations to cover my absence from Fishers Retirement Residence, aka my house. I processed the pile of orders that had accumulated on my desk, well those that were in danger of falling off the edge anyway. Malcolm would, in due course, return, documents in hand, querying why the order for Switzerland had ten dining chairs and no table and the Finnish order demanded a custom-made sideboard longer than a stretch limousine. Malcolm was also stock control; work in hand manager and quality control. It was a task he took on off his own bat as, when things went wrong, he was the one who took all the crabby phone calls. He was also the one who provided me with an alibi.

'Dennis,' I said 'you'll never guess what?'

'W-w-w what?' said Dennis.

'I've got to go on a business trip.'

'W-w-why?'

'Well, because the boss has decided that I'm going to follow through my work dealing with the export side,' I said proudly, and convincingly I hoped.

'W-w-where are you going?'

'France.'

'W-w-when?'

'Saturday,' I informed him; thank goodness it wasn't W-W-W-Warsaw on a W-W-W-Wednesday.

'Oh right, will you be shopping before you go then? We'll need some frozen dinners.' His major problems, that of his stomach and caring full time for his mother, appeared gratified by my cheerful, 'yes, of course, and I'll leave you some steamed puddings too,' which lulled him into an albeit false sense of security. He had forgotten that he might miss the footie if required for household duties. Thankfully however, the subject of a passport or apparent lack of said document didn't rear its ugly head.

TWENTY- FOUR

Aries: Your feelings are in danger of running away with you. Are you prepared to compete in this race? Do you want to?

The ferry chugged away from Portsmouth with me, staring from a windswept deck, at the receding twinkling coastline prickling with excitement, clutching my passport in the depths of my pocket. I couldn't wait to meet my first Frenchman; I really hoped he had on a stripy tee shirt and a beret. I wanted to savour my first real French meal too. I drew the line at snails obviously.

'Come on Lynda, we're going to the bar,' shouted Lorraine 'You're missing valuable duty-free drinking time.'

'But it's six o'clock in the morning,' I protested.

'Oh well,' said Lorraine. 'It's nine pm in Tokyo (probably). Come on.'

Several hours later I stood alone again; windswept and damp watching this foreign continent coming into view through hovering grey clouds. I sniffed the air, watching the white foamy water bouncing around, wondering if the seagulls that had suddenly appeared understood French or English. A gang of gum chewing animated schoolchildren appeared with a weary, prematurely balding teacher. I drank in their enthusiasm and shivered, eagerly sharing their anticipation.

'Right you lot, it's raining so I suggest you all go indoors with Mrs. Guscott and get into your wet weather gear,' the lilting welsh voice announced, 'We'll be landing soon.'

'But we don't want to be with Mrs. Gusset, we want to be with you,' wailed a waif like blonde. As a chorus of voices reached fever pitch he suddenly snapped.

'Enough, get inside, sit down and behave,' he barked. I was pleased to see that this inspired a max exodus of shuffling youngsters.

'Well, you can certainly keep them in check, I'm impressed.'

'It's amazing what you can achieve when you want a fag;' he smiled pulling cigarettes and lighter from his top pocket.

'Do you smoke?' He proffered the packet; I shook my head. I had never socialized with a teacher before, I was overcome, me talking to a teacher — and not at parents evening trying to justify why I hadn't noticed the boys not doing their homework. Whilst I struggled to sustain the conversation, he visibly relaxed now he was on his own, drawing long and hard on his B & H and in the time it took to dock the ferry I learned of his recent divorce, his mother's cooking and his love of horse riding. He, on the other hand, knew very little about me, well there was nothing to tell was there? Except the fact that I was now looking forward to having my passport stamped, thereby proving my status as an explorer. In different circumstances I might have been drawn to this handsome, educated and I thought underneath passionate man and there was clearly an infatuation bubbling between us. We stood gazing at each other for several minutes, not needing to talk, before we both remembered our responsibilities. His, a herd of pubescent juveniles, were now looking at him and jeering through the fogged-up windows of the lounge and he pulled away from my side.

'You'd think we were having rampant sex looking at them, wouldn't you?' Their gesticulations appeared to confirm his assumptions and we grinned at one another.

'I wish,' I heard myself say, before blushing deeply and hiccupping loudly.

'Look at my lot then,' I said quickly indicating the bar area. Looking through the double doors it was clear that the girls were still being entertained by Malcolm's salacious repertoire of jokes in the bar. Loud cackles interspersed his low monotonous tones, I almost wished I hadn't come. Trying to fight off his amorous advances at six am had been a low point on an otherwise thrilling day. I'd eaten croissants while the others had tucked into full English. They had tea and I had a large bowl of hot chocolate. I could just see Ivy's face if I proffered her French cuisine.

'That the gang you're with is it?' asked Peter 'they look fun.'

'Um yes, they are I suppose. But I don't think we'll be doing any sightseeing; they want to go to the hypermarkets.'

'I expect my lot would do, given half a chance. But we're heading for Paris now. The Arc de Triomphe, the Louvre, the crème of sophistication and elegance – a cultural epicentre but they'll be complaining of aching feet and hiding in corners texting their mates back

158

home. I'd much rather be with you. I'd love to give you the guided tour (for I had confessed I had never been to Paris before) – we could share so much.' Was he going to ask for my number, did he want to see me again? I speculated, blushing madly. Or is he just teasing? But I would never know because at that moment Malcolm chose to descend on me, placing both hands on my chest in a very familiar fashion shouting 'Beep Beep.' My rosy glow turned to turnip red and I looked around, but Peter had gone, he'd been swallowed in a sea of anoraks, school bags and chatter. As I touched French soil, I felt an urge to drop down and kiss the ground, but I managed to resist the temptation. I waved my passport around looking in vain for a slight Frenchman with peaked round cap and small moustache holding a rubber stamp, until Polly told me 'Put it away, you're a European now.'

'Wow,' I thought, 'Yeah right,' I replied, anxious to hide my excitement, for it didn't do with these young people to show enthusiasm. I didn't want them to realize I was old and sad. My eyes darted everywhere trying to drink in the atmosphere, my ears pricked craving every snippet of French conversation, although of course I hadn't a clue what they were saying. Memories of secondary school came flooding back; things could have been so different. Miss Briffitt had made us stand in line in the hall; I remember her holding a big bundle of exam papers. As our names were read out, we had walked to the front to stand under her beady gaze. She read my percentages out loud, and looking over the top of her half-rimmed spectacles pointed me in the direction of the needlework room. My destiny was decided then, no modern languages or science for me, for I was going to make an apron and cook toad in the hole.

'Come on Lynda,' said Donna, tucking her arm in mine, 'We're off to Carrefour.' I could feel my Euros jingling, and I put up my 'parapluie' (I knew that because my new M & S one had dual labelling), and trotted down the road shouting 'Bonjour' to every passer-by. Time passed all too quickly, and before long I was back on the ferry throwing up. Nobody else was ill, perhaps I should have followed their example and headed straight to the bar. Still, even with all the excesses of lunch, French sticks, croissants and, I feel an orgasm coming on, mouth-watering, scrumptious, French chocolate éclairs. But on the plus side I should have lost at least three pounds at this rate. I looked in the speckled cabin mirror, my face was thinner, but following down my body I could see that my face's loss was my middles gain. Nita, now desperate to advertise her pregnancy was pushing it all out whilst I was condemned to posing boobs out, stomach in, bottom tucked under at all times whilst out in public. It was only in my greenhouse that I could really relax and let it all hang out. As I opened my front door I was overwhelmed by the smell of vinegar, oh no!

'Hello, had a good time?' Mums soaking the onions in the bath, but it'll only be for a day or two. Bring back anything nice?' I unpacked the various cheeses and salamis to show Dennis, but the aroma was rather overwhelming in a confined area and he wrinkled his nose untrusting of this foreign stuff I was trying to pass off as food.

'What's wrong with a bit of Cheddar then?' he sniffed. I packed it into the fridge; well I was going to enjoy it, so there. Well, I think I will, some of it does look a little strange though, and it was a bit of a lottery with French labels! Polly thought I might have bought horsemeat. No, I couldn't see it myself. I felt wretched and headed for the bathroom. After I had been sick yet again, I twisted the rubber shower spray over the loo to wash my hair and contented myself with a rub down with a flannel. How many pounds of onions has she done I wondered glancing into the half-filled bath - enough to see her out I thought spitefully. Oh well, back to the real world.

TWENTY- FIVE

I'm learning Japanese, I'm learning Japanese, I do hope so.

'Mrs. Fisher, my office – five minutes, please' boomed a distant thundering voice.

'Oooooooh' chanted Cheryl, 'Mr. Manley calls, what you think he wants with you Lynda?'

'I've no idea,' I replied 'But I'm going to the ladies first.' I grabbed my handbag, delving deeply inside the cavernous interior for my makeup bag. Mandy and Lolly joined me for a girlie chat and we balanced leaning over the wash hand basins, to get closer to the mirrors applying lipstick, straightening skirts, and pulling wayward bras back into place. We could have been the Beverley sisters, I decided, but didn't say it just in case they stared inanely and asked 'Who?'

'Bet he's going to offer you a raise,' advised Mandy.

'Yeah he's only got to see you and he thinks about a raise, if you know what I mean.' I narrowly dodged one of Lolly's bone crunching sideways elbowing hugs.

The last time I was there, in his office, the hallowed inner sanctum, I had quivered, nervous, irresolute, facing his walrus features feeling inferior, insignificant. Looking in the mirror today I could see a changed woman, and I realized how far I had come, how much I had changed in six months. No wonder Dennis was struggling, his little mouse had crawled out from under the stone and turned into…. I growled at my reflection, seeing the tiger within, making my colleagues jump.

'Lynda, my lippy's now half way up my nose thanks to you.'

'Do you think I've changed since I've been here?' I turned to face the two early twenty something's

'Transformed more like,' said Mandy, 'your jokes are filthy now, and you can drink me under the table.'

'That wasn't quite what I meant,' I laughed, but I was impressed all the same.

'Well, you were an old frump when you came here,' she added enthusiastically, and now look at you - showing off your stocking tops ready to persuade the old man to promote you.' I pulled down my skirt protectively.

'I did not wear those for him,' I protested, 'because I didn't know he wanted to see me, did I?'

'So, who are they for?' quizzed Mandy. 'That's for me to know and you not to find out,' I giggled, but a rose-tinted vision of Peter, in a gown and mortar – and only that – with his enquiring face ogling me over half rimmed glasses floated past me. I could almost touch him. I blushed as the image, one hand outstretched, flinched slightly as a deftly aimed ruler, held in the other hand, flicked his open palm.

'You have been a naughty girl haven't you?' Peter was mouthing. I could read his lips so well.

'God, Lynda, you can't walk into his office with your nipples poking out like that, he may offer you a better job, but he may not live to authorize the payments to the accounts department.'

'Who are you thinking about anyway, it's not that sales rep from yesterday is it? The one who dropped his propelling pen down your lacy halter neck?'

'No, of course it isn't,' I snapped, remembering the fuss Dennis had made about the ink stains over my boobs last night. And he had a few choice words to say about the top too.

'If I'd seen that in Tesco's,' he had complained 'I'd have told them it wasn't strong enough to hold grapes let alone a couple of ripe melons.' And he had reached out to me; cupping me in his workman's hands. And we had made love, I as a dutiful wife and he as exciting as a Lego man. My attempts to spice up our sex life had been stubbornly declined.

'No Mother might hear us,' was his first excuse, swiftly followed by 'I've got work tomorrow', or when I was too pushy, a sharp, I'd do my bloody back in and then where will we be?' You'd have thought he would have been thrilled, but no, he didn't like change. He was the same about the bathroom. I'd pleaded 'but I'd like a new bathroom, perhaps we could fit in a shower too?' You would have thought I'd asked for a urinal and sun bed by the sharp intake of breath.

'Lynda, hadn't you better go see the old man?' nagged Mandy, bringing me back from yet another daydream.

'Yes- O.K. I'm going,' I said, tweaking my skirt. As I slunk along the corridor, well aware that he would be watching my every move on closed circuit television I was still puzzled as to what he could want. He wasn't thinking of sacking me, was he? It wasn't my fault that Tom in dispatch had problems with his pacemaker, and

I'd tried to practice my first aid when he fell to the ground gasping for air. I'd loosened his collar, put him in the recovery position and called for an ambulance. As his colour had returned, I'd sat him up a little resting his head on my chest, trying to ensure his airways remained clear. But that had seemed to aggravate his condition and I felt helpless. I could only pat his head and offer reassurance – but it didn't sound genuine. Should I tell Mr. Manley I would like to go on a First Aid Course? I jumped as he appeared at his door, and with a grand gesture he invited me in. I sat down, crossing my legs trying to look super-efficient. Mr. Manly used both his dumpy arms to propel him back into his large leather director's chair.

'Well,' he said smiling. My phone rang out with the tune that meant it could only be Peter.

'Sorry,' I said, reaching for my handbag, flicking my phone open.

'No, I can't talk now, I'll phone you later. Yes, I know its break time; can't you skip games or something?' I added irritably. Mr. Manly smiled indulgently,

'Children are a problem aren't they, always wanting something, I know my little Lucy pestered me day and night until I got her a fishing rod.' Thank god he doesn't know this child is forty-six! I thought, feeling a hot flush coming on. I couldn't tell him that the last thing my younger son asked me for was a donation towards a phone bill for his 0900 numbers! His smile had faded slightly at my continued silence, 'Tea Mrs. Fisher?'

'Um. Thanks, yes please.' He buzzed Maureen, his personal bimbo.

'Tea please, for two, and don't forget the biscuits, the Rich Tea's please.' He wasn't aware that it was common knowledge on the factory floor that a group of Japanese businessmen had been presented with Jammie Dodgers and Iced Gems in the boardroom. But we got the order so who knows, perhaps you need to cast off the traditions in business to stay on top. Oh, dear he was talking, what was I missing?

I managed to spill my tea and the conversation died as he watched the trickle of liquid disappear down my cleavage. He hopped off his chair and produced a giant white handkerchief — so large I almost expected a rabbit to pop out. He pawed successfully at my front, removing every trace.

'Well shall we get to the point?' he said, wiping his now sweating face with the hankie. My phone rang out again

'Damn, sorry, sorry.' This time I flicked it onto voice mail, and silent, and tried to concentrate.

'Well, Mrs. Fisher, you've been with for some considerable time now, and I must say we at Manley's Traditional Furniture Company are very pleased with your work. You're very popular with your colleagues, and we like to think that we can recognize...'

'Oh just get on with it,' I wanted to scream. I'd promised to take Nita to antenatal.

'Of course, I have taken advice from your immediate boss who...'

'Oh come on,' my stomach was churning now, what was he going to offer me?

'Oh no.'

'I'm so sorry,' I said fleeing his office, trying desperately to hold back the sickness, at least until I was out the office. I was never going to drink red wine again. Thankfully I reached the executive washroom- well needs must. Whilst I was being sick down the toilet, I felt this amazing quivering over my heart and clutched at my breast, fortunately quickly grasping the fact that it was my mobile's vibration only mode.

'Peter not now,' I managed to say before throwing up again. I felt immediately better and re applied my make up after freshening my face with cold water. Meekly now I knocked on Mr. Manley's office door. It was opened by Miss Butterworth.

'Ah Mrs. Fisher, are you feeling better now?' she enquired, barely moving her pursed lips?

'I'm so sorry,' I explained 'my daughter in law is pregnant you know, I think it's sympathy pains!' The gruesome twosome looked steadily at the floor. Well, I thought, that shut them up. The girls in the office were right, just talk about hormones or girly things and you can get away with murder.

'Well, shall we resume our conversation Mrs. Fisher, or may I call you Liz?'

'You're the boss, Mr. Manley you can call me anything you want, but I probably won't answer,' I giggled

'I'm Lynda.' He had to decency to redden and after a few coughs and heruumps launched into a conversation that would justify my very existence.

'Well then - we have a chance to compete in the world market,' he said proudly, 'and to that end I have to go to Japan in a month or two to show off our products. And the thing is Lynda,' he hollered 'I'd like you to come and show off your assets too.' Now it was Miss Butterworth's turn to splutter into her teacup, whilst I just sat open mouthed.

'But doesn't Miss Thomas usually accompany you on these trips? I asked.

'Yes, yes of course, but as you know she's into amateur dramatics and she's got a very big role in the Mikado around that time, and she...' But his words were lost in the rush of exhilaration that left me tingling, wondering if I was going to wet myself or be catapulted into outer space with the force of total ecstasy.

'Yes, yes, and yes,' I shrieked, hopping, skipping and jumping through the shag pile, recklessly and without a moment's consideration for professionalism.

'Yes, right then, we'll leave the details till later then,' agreed a totally flummoxed Mr. Manley. Back once again in the safety of the washrooms I sat on the loo, picked up my phone, wondering who to tell first. I just had to tell someone. I flicked through my text messages.

What have I done wrong? PETER

What's the matter? PETER

Talk to me! PETER

Remember it was you who, impatiently I pressed the more button, who suggested the ruler.

I pressed delete all, and returned to the office – waiting until I had captured everyone's attention before casually asking 'Has anyone got a guidebook for Japan they can lend me?'

168

For the first time ever in my whole life I was the centre of attention. They all wanted to know all the details, not that I knew them yet, and I faced a barrage of questions which I started to answer. The answers though inspired more questions so, with a grand gesture I waved, opened the door and as a parting shot announced 'I'll tell you the rest, in The Spotted Dick, I'm buying.' I floated down the corridor with a grin fit for a Cheshire cat.

TWENTY- SIX

Aries: Tackle problems head on- there may be mayhem but some progress too.

I retreated to the greenhouse; idly plucking parched leaves from the neglected geraniums - their faded, wilting blooms mirroring my existence. I'd made such giant leaps in the last few months but now my world was falling apart. Dennis wasn't talking to me, and neither was his mother. Stupidly I'd thought they would have been as elated as I was, a chance to fly to Japan, all expenses paid, and it was only for one week for god's sake, I'd snapped. But as far as they were concerned their world had fallen apart - they had lost their cook and washer up, their cleaner, their lifeline apparently. Nita told me not to worry- that they would come round - eventually, but I didn't think so. I'd gone too far this time. Even the boys had taken their fathers side. And there was no escape at work either; for not everyone was happy with my swift promotion. I was even accused of sleeping my way to Japan. Stupid really, as most of them would have taken that option were it open to them. But I hadn't, I didn't need to - I got the results I wanted by being good at my job. I cared about my job, and they didn't. And the thought of sleeping with Mr. Manley – well it was just gross. Something small and brown scuttled past with Des in quick pursuit and I grabbed him, anxious to prevent the needless lingering death of a harmless little mouse. I scooped him up - held him close and received a sharp painful scratch. I peered down my front looking at the wound. Even he was seeking retribution now, for usually he would just snuggle in, purring loudly. He struggled to escape with tail swishing wildly, wide eyes and menacing growl. I felt his friendship oozing away with the blood now staining my t-shirt. My stars this morning had warned me of getting out of my depth, and I supposed that Dennis would accuse me of a torrid affair now- sighting a six-inch wound from a careless lover as evidence. I peered down at it, placing Des none too gently on the ground. Could it be mistaken for signs of passion? Probably, I thought, but as my lover was only in my head this was not a possibility. The stinging was irritating, disturbing my deepest thoughts and I decided I should probably head for the first aid box. But that would mean entering no man's land – the kitchen - so I looked for an alternative. I picked up a soil-encrusted scalpel, turning it over and over, would the lack of an antiseptic wipe necessitate a tetanus injection when infection set in. Did it matter so much – I was Mrs. No-Mates at the moment and feeling very sorry for myself? With an unexpected burst of enthusiasm, I lunged at an adjacent Aloe Vera plant hacking off a plump leaf. I quickly applied the oozing substance onto my cut, and then watched the wounded plant leaking. It's probably crying I decided. Des, tiring now of watching a tiny mouse holed up in a flowerpot begged for a cuddle.

'All forgiven,' I said, 'and whatever you hear said about me isn't true, Des, you've got to believe me. I did not sleep with Godfrey Manley; no one could be that desperate,' I whispered. 'And there's that business of

171

Peter too. Des you understand don't you, I just wanted a bit of fun, and you can't be guilty of having an affair over the phone, can you? All that business of Peter with his gown on and nothing else, well it's just make believe. I only sent text messages with my fantasies Des. Besides he told me that since his wife left him, well, it's left him with a problem, you know what I mean don't you Des?' He purred loudly, seemingly nodding his head in answer. I continued tickling his neck, delving deep underneath his collar. He wriggled and stretched a frenzy of excitement and when he reached a pinnacle of stimulation his whole body quivered starting at his whiskers, ending at the tip of his tail. I held him tightly.

'Oh Des, if only someone could that for me.' I heard feeble, uneven footsteps and ducked down, slithering under the staging, anxious to avoid Ivy as she passed by with the washing basket to peg out her smalls.

'Smalls Des, her knickers are the size of dustbin liners.' I slid my free hand down between my legs feeling for mine - scarlet silky skimpy ones with ribbon ties at each side. I'd described them to Peter by text message. Pushing Des into a sunny corner, I reached for my phone and re-read his reply now.

Having a hard day, let's hope it continues! Love Peter xxx.

Dennis, on the other hand, despite being offered hands on experience last night had turned back to his Railway News Bumper Edition, muttering 'At your age you should...' but his words were lost as I fled to the front room immersing myself in an Open University programme on economics in the Soviet Union. I

172

watched, from my hiding place, Dennis pushing his bike down the path, bicycle clips at the ready.

'Bye mum, off to do a spot of fishing, when Lynda gets back from the shops tell her will you?'

'That's right son, you have a nice time, and I'll tell Lynda to have tea ready for six.'

'That's if I see her,' she muttered as she passed right by me, the green gauze erected to protect the cucumbers from the searing July sun, protecting me too. If I closed my eyes I could almost believe I was on a faraway deserted beach. I could hear water, a distant lapping – probably Des in the cat bowl, and smell the coconuts — from my body moisturizer, but in my daydream, I could see the swaying trees behind me. I slipped off my t-shirt and skirt and stretched out on the sand-covered floor drinking in the hot sun. Drenched with sweat I kept my eyes shut tightly, dreaming fleetingly of Peter, then a stranger, feeling only intense pleasure. Having been deeply dissatisfied with my forecast in the daily paper I had turned to one in a glossy magazine which advised me to retreat into my own world and find solace. I wasn't quite sure what solace was but I'd definitely found satisfaction, but now the sun was moving around and I was feeling chilly all of a sudden. Des was hassling me for tea and I had to find a way to get back into the house devoid of plastic shopping bags. And what the hell could I cook for tea? What was left in the freezer? Tried and trusted recipe, traditional, boring needed – NOW.

'Sod the world and his wife,' I thought as I peeled the potatoes ripping their skins off, dropping them back into the water, splashing the sink, the drainer and me.

I've done nothing wrong, but I am going to Japan, and I will go to the reunion next month. And I'll meet up with Sally, the trolley dolly, and refuse to be intimidated by Verity Osborne-Box, the Channel Four presenter, and keep trying to find out what Julie Andrews has to hide. I have a life too. And as I chopped the potatoes into chips, I wondered whether to go against all the rules and try to arrange a meet beforehand with some of the girls. I could strut my stuff with the best of them now. As I dropped the potatoes into the sizzling fat Dennis appeared holding a cool box.

'Aah fresh fish for tea is it?' I smiled. He opened the lid and I peered inside to see a neat row of blue ice boxes. I shrugged my shoulders, 'just as well I defrosted the sausages then.'

TWENTY- SEVEN

Gemini: Your elders may need your help. They just don't know it yet.

I was on autopilot cooking the tea, shifting the positions of the smouldering sausages at monotonous intervals. Only the persistent ringing of the phone brought me back to the real world, but I chose to ignore it anyway. Glancing through the serving hatch I saw the oh so deaf one knitting and Dennis watching football. I decided to let 1571 do its job. My stomach was churning, though regrettably it was out completely out of sync with my throbbing head. As one of the sausages split its skin, its insipid innards bubbled out lazily and I named it Lynda, for it was me. My fluctuating weight was spiralling out of control. I had acquired teenage spots and a craving for anything with zillions of calories and no redeeming features such as Glusomine Sulphate, whatever that was. I unhooked the button and loosened the zip on my jeans – let it all hang out I thought despondently. I poked and prodded the sausages, sporadically flipping them over, and by the time the chips were cooked they had all acquired identities. The big lumpy one was Nita. I can't believe I'm going to be a grandmother. I'm not ready for this, I thought, stabbing it violently, and then suffered immediate guilt pangs. Is voodoo real or not? I withdrew my fork carefully choosing instead to harass the puny, shrivelled sausage cowering between two hefty bangers. It was all going wrong, tears welled up and I mopped them with the corner of the tea towel. Taking a deep, snivelling breath I served the meal, placing them on the trays ready for collection. The phone rang again, and as it was half time, Dennis shot off to answer it.

'Hello, it's three nil isn't that brill?' he said, before ascertaining that it was his mate Les phoning to book a celebration drink with the lads tonight, 'cos obviously we're going to win, now aren't we?' I heard him boasting. I slid his plate back under the grill when I realised, he had parked himself on the bottom stair, a sure sign he was going to natter until kick off. Oh well, I could blame the burnt offerings on him then, couldn't I?

Mother-in-law came to collect hers as soon as her walking stick, wielded by me, touched her shoulder. I must check her hearing aid for batteries again; I bet she's taken them out to save power. I watched as she pointed the remote at the TV pressing the buttons extra hard - I guess they need new batteries too, I sighed. I decided to eat in the relative peace of the kitchen, where I could read my cherished mail uninterrupted. The envelope proudly proclaimed Channel 4 — the people's channel. Which people I didn't know - refugee's maybe. I'd heard they had satellite and golf lessons in their welcome to Britain package. You will be pleased to hear, it stated, that we have set a date for the reunion, and we enclose a list of participants for your perusal, including previous names of course. Oh yes, of course, because I knew one girl who was now on her fourth marriage and then there was Julie who retained her stage name, not forgetting fly me Mandy

176

who just wanted to retain her independence. Well, if I needed an excuse to get back on the diet here it was, less than a month away now. Two pounds a week minimum — that's half a stone and back into my thin wardrobe. My fork cluttered on the floor, closely followed by my plate, sausages, chips and the peas. I'd just noticed the date, the day after I was due to fly out to Japan. Wouldn't you just know it, forty years of sod all and now I was confronted with a see saw of opportunity. My brain screamed conflicting instructions. Past or future – beginnings or conclusions? I could hear Dennis in the background as I sat there with a lap full of peas and a tortured expression.

'Well of course,' he was saying, 'Lynda has to go on a business trip to Japan later this month, so we can't accept your invitation to a barbeque until the dates are firmed up, but we could pencil in a possible date if you like.' The voice was his, the turn of phrase pinched from some sales executive at work probably.

'She'll have a lot to tell us, won't she?' The pride in his voice was unmistakable, I couldn't believe I was hearing this, why hadn't he told me he was pleased for me?

'Oh yes - she's flying out from London, business class, with her boss, they'll be staying in a four, maybe five-star hotel, who would have thought it eh? I'm tickled pink you know. Got to go, the footies back on. See you later.' I watched with gaping mouth as he scuttled back to his cosy armchair.

'I'll have some coffee when you're ready Lynda,' he yelled. I flicked the kettle on and went to phone Nita.

We were due for another check-up, well she was anyway, and she wouldn't go without me. She'd gone really strange. As I picked up the phone the tell-tale beep alerting me - one message received; I pressed to hear it.

'Hello it's Gladys, are you there Ivy? Are you there? Oh I can't speak to these answering thingies, you'll have to phone me back. It's really exciting about your Lynda isn't it? Japan, I can't believe it. Your Lynda becoming a plane spotter, that's what they call them isn't it? You must be really excited? I hope she'll bring you back something nice. They're really small over there aren't they? And you'd better tell her not to talk about the war. Can you hear me Ivy, oh blow, see you at the centre; it's liver and onions tomorrow. Bye.' So, she was pleased for me too, god, like mother like son, and I had thought they didn't give a toss. The phone rang immediately I placed the receiver down.

'Hello, you'll never believe it — our Malcolm's been signed off sick with R.S.I. I had to laugh, just wait till he's back on the shop floor.'

'But that's not funny Lorraine, I bet it really hurts. Is it an industrial injury?'

'No, definitely domestic, if you know what I mean,' she chortled. 'It's his wrist you see, and how do you think he got it?' She snorted loudly and I suddenly got her drift.

'No,' I purred.

'Oh yes,' she retorted.

TWENTY- EIGHT

Aries: There is light on the horizon and a New Moon on Friday!

Fantastic news awaited me when I went back to work - the trip to Japan had been re-scheduled and I could now attend both the get-together, and the business trip. I had emailed Channel Four immediately, accepting their generous offer of a long weekend with, admittedly, three-star accommodation and, after glancing only briefly at their contract, had signed with a flourish and posted back the documents. I was now officially a participant in their reality TV show the Class of 67 Reunion. And I was going to Japan the following week – a corporate, fact finding, sales opportunity trip. Oh, I knew that it was only Mr. Manley flogging furniture but it sounds fantastic if you don't elaborate, I decided. I needed a visa apparently and a phonetic translation of my name into Japanese for introductions. I sincerely hoped Lynda Fisher would sound better in Japanese. It was almost bound to be wasn't it? Excitement made my body quiver, and I panted, blushed profusely   sending all the wrong signals to my portly boss.

'Oh, and by the way,' explained Mr. Manley, staring at me, now keen to prolong the conversation, 'Um, don't mention the number four in Japan, it's very unlucky there apparently.' I wondered briefly how we were going to get over selling dining tables with sets of four chairs which were on our best-selling list now. I asked the question.

'In Japan, my dear we will sell table, three chairs and one carver,' he elucidated, slithering closer to me, invading my personal space.

'Right, I see,' I replied, backing off, making my exit with blazing cheeks and a wiggle liable to topple me from my much-loved high heels. I could hear him panting like a cocker spaniel as I entered the lift to leave the executive suite and return to my floor, only one floor up from despatch. I hadn't even asked Mr. Manley why the Japanese were ordering our furniture. In all the films I had seen they were sitting on the floor, legs crossed. The last time I did that was in Jamaica Street Infants. Their tables were the height of our coffee tables. I shrugged; I supposed they could always cut the legs down if they didn't like them. My diary, which up to the beginning of this year had been a testimonial to my commitment to a monotonous marriage, was now bulging with events, past, present and even future. It remained hidden from prying eyes in the inner lining of my handbag, my Monday to Friday one that is. At weekends I dispersed with the cavernous hold all and charged around with a little pink number designed to hold lipstick and a credit card. The girls, of course, also squashed into theirs a packet of condoms and travelling toothbrush. I used the available space to carry Paracetemol, library tickets and a four leaved clover key ring, set in plastic resin. It was less than a month until the reunion and I still had unfulfilled cravings which I needed to satisfy in order to complete my total reinvention of my past. Six months of fabricating   a lifetime of experiences had passed - a manic mix of fun, work and begrudged moments of boredom. My stomach churned at the thought of meeting all my old school friends, offering my past up on a plate. Would it stand up to close scrutiny or would I be portrayed, exposed even to Channel Four viewers as a middle-aged housewife standing on the edge of life.

'How much longer are you going to be in there?' came a whinging cry from Dennis? An irritated thump on the loo door followed as I ignored his appeal. Well, you can't answer when your head is shoved down the toilet and you're throwing up can you?

'I told you it was asking for trouble eating at that Chinese restaurant, didn't I? Didn't I tell you Lynda?' I groaned a response, flushed the loo, splashed my face with cold water, trying, but not succeeding to avoid damaging my carefully applied eye makeup. With dogged persistence Dennis continued to talk through the yellowed white gloss door.

'I suppose I'm making my own sandwiches, again am I?' he complained. 'Again?'

I thought heaving, 'Since when?'

'And had you forgotten that Mother wanted to take a plate of sausage rolls to her whist drive today?' I whined, loudly, hoping for a sympathetic response.

'Oh, and Lynda, could you pick up a seed catalogue on your way home, I'm off to the allotment members club meeting tonight.' I gave up being ill, and slid the bolt back. Head held high I headed for the kitchen. I opened the fridge, eyes scurrying over the contents, yes, there it was, that pot of sardine spread Ivy had won at the Tuesday club. If he wanted sandwiches, he could have them, he hated sardines. Taking a deep breath whilst unscrewing the lid, I retched only slightly. But it was worth it to think what he would suffer when he took that first bite. I filled a Tupperware container with packets of salted peanuts, pork scratchings and Bombay mix. I held it out to the oh so deaf one who was propped up in the corner by her tartan wheeled shopping trolley.

'Here you are Mother,' I shouted, rattling the box, 'I thought it would be a change from sausage rolls.'

'There's no need to shout,' she said grumpily, 'I'm not deaf' tapping her hearing aid against the worktop. As she peered inside the box, I hid my face in the pantry, supposedly foraging for some new batteries.

'Lynda, you know these get under my plate, what are you thinking of?' I grinned for I was peeking at a gaggle of wrinkly old ladies with gummy grimaces and tooth picks in my mind. I walked to work bathed in watery sunshine, under clear blue skies shaking off my early morning woes as the trees were shedding the last drops of overnight dew. With every step I grew an inch. At five foot one I often felt insignificant, but I was going to Japan. There surely, I would feel more conspicuous. I'd be regular height, possibly on the tall side of petite there. Excitement buzzed through my entire body, this was better than an orgasm, well, the ones I'd had anyway.

TWENTY- NINE

Aries: Your priorities will change many times this year.
A rolling stone….

I lay in bed mentally preparing myself for the weekly trip to Tesco's. Milk, yoghurt, oh, mustn't forget the sausage rolls for his lunchbox, nor the soft mints for the oh so deaf one. Not for the first time I wished I had a ready prepared list for this was no time to reach for a pen and paper, and my attention kept wandering back to the   conversation I'd had with Lorraine and Cilla whilst enjoying a quick half in the Spotted Dick, it being pay day. Dennis groaned softly bringing me abruptly back to the present. I shouldn't feel like this, I must pay attention. I rubbed his shoulder, tenderly, I hoped.   Dennis murmured, 'Oh that's nice' like he always did. Cadburys cocoa, I mustn't forget that, it was a godsend when Ivy couldn't sleep. Mogodon can be stirred in surreptitiously I'd found. Dennis moved into act two of his set routine and I had to groan a little, as usual, so that he could continue. And I went back to my day dream.

'Sky diving?' I'd said incredulously, nearly choking on my Bacardi, in reply to Cilla's suggestion last week.

'For charity,' she'd continued.

'With a parachute?' I'd queried.

'No, with a duvet cover, you daft cow. Of course, with a parachute - and with a big strong fella strapped to your backside.'

'How's that work?'

'It's called a tandem skydive - you hook onto this instructor in the plane and he jumps with you.'

'From what height?' I asked, although why I don't know because anything over the height of my front room was beyond my comprehension. I remembered the difficulties of visualizing stopping distances, wet road, dry road and all that on my driving lessons. Oops, he's groaning again. I patted Dennis on his bald patch and he hummed happily.

'Ten thousand feet the bumph said,' affirmed Cilla, adding knowledgeably, '120 miles per hour, freefall, takes about thirty seconds to hit the ground apparently.'

'And you do it for charity.'

'Yep, you get sponsors, at least three hundred pounds worth and then you get to do it for free and the charity gets the dosh.'

'Sounds ok I think,' I had heard myself saying 'Scary but okay.'

'I'm doing it definitely,' Cilla had said, 'I'm doing it for breast cancer' she added, thrusting her enormous chest in the direction of the despatch lads. 'You'll sponsor me won't you?' she grinned cheekily. It still amazed me that though she saw them every day she could still get them to dribble on command. They'd all licked their lips and nodded stupidly.

'Only if you do it topless,' suggested Garry.

'Hey, great idea, Lynda, we'll all do it topless, what a laugh.' Cilla retorted. I saw myself, sky high, bared breasts cupped by a hunky instructor's sun kissed hands and felt a surge of enthusiasm. A formidable 'Oh,' slipped out of my mouth, before I could stop it.

'Bout time,' said Dennis, 'I thought you'd dropped off for a minute,' and he shuddered momentarily as he climaxed. I hugged him, murmuring I love you. Dental floss, mustn't forget that either I thought, noticing the stringy green beans wedged between his crooked bottom teeth.

'I love you too; d-don't leave me Lynda, will you? I couldn't go on without you.'

'Don't be daft Dennis, I've no intention of leaving you — or your mother,' I added with gritted teeth. As Dennis gently snored beside me, I considered the meaning of life, well mine anyway. A year ago, I was not unhappy, just gloomier, with a humdrum future, boring, unfulfilling and totally predictable. I had looked on Dennis as a responsibility, along with his mother and my children, who though they had left home were still a major part of my life. How things had changed, and now my life was so full I needed a page a day diary to keep up with it all. My mind was awash with all the things I had done and all the things I had left to do, Japan was coming up soon, my visa had arrived today. I was going to fit in the skydiving too. I let my hands creep over my breasts and stomach. Not topless for me then, for realistically I knew I couldn't hold my stomach in for a 10,000-foot freefall. I looked over at Dennis, laying on his back, mouth open snuffling and suddenly felt awash with love. My eyes filled unexpectedly with tears. It could only be the menopause I decided for my emotions were all over the place. I'd read all the magazines in readiness. Maybe it was time to make an appointment with the Doctor to get HRT or something. These mood swings did not fit it my lifestyle at all and needed sorting. I might be expecting my first grandchild but I had my dream list too and crying one moment and giggling outrageously the next were definitely not on the agenda. Dennis shifted in his sleep, taking in a deep breath, exhaling with quivering lips and his now shrivelled willy popped out from his Marks and Sparks pyjama bottoms. I mentally added on pyjama cord to my shopping list then crossed it off immediately - substituting boxer shorts black, Kelvin Klein. He shifted onto his front, exposing the top quarter of a sagging rump and, then as he continued his 360-degree rollover, a belly a certain breed of pig would be pleased to possess. Maybe not the boxers then, I smiled. I settled down curling into him, and dreamed of Japan, where I miraculously became tall, blonde and willowy, and of skydiving, fearlessly, before abandoning my parachute in favour of a raft where I was attempting the world record for white water rafting down the Niagara Falls.

Saturdays were always a disappointment as routine bit firmly into my dream world. Shopping first thing, after making Dennis his cooked breakfast which was a prerequisite for a long day on the allotment. Ivy had to be dropped off at the hairdressers on the way; her blue rinse needed a boost. I plodded round Tesco's getting the same old stuff for the same old meals, I dithered around the Italian section wondering if cannelloni might be sneaked onto the menu but decided reluctantly that it couldn't be served with gravy and would therefore be unacceptable. I looked for a section labelled Japanese, but didn't find one so picked up a large Cadburys Dairy Milk to take with me, just in case. I made up my mind to try everything I was offered in Tokyo, baby octopus, whatever - even if it was raw, as I was sure that to decline would cause offence. The clothing section offered me the boxer shorts I had in mind for Dennis, but I hesitated again. Instead I plumped for some new knickers for me, lacy and alluring. If my bag was going to be searched by customs by any chance, I wanted to be proud of my underwear. Oh, and batteries, most important. If I was going for a week, I would need some double A's for my vibrator, but I wavered again doubting that my Deluxe Pleasurometer would pass as a torch by customs officials should my bag be searched. Maybe I should get a new one of those too, something very discreet. I'd send Cilla out looking for one next week, I didn't have the nerve to loiter doing window shopping - let alone venture inside. I filled a second trolley with party bits, for tonight was to be a family affair. Thank goodness I could drive now, before I had either struggled on the bus, or had to phone Dennis, dragging him reluctantly away from his seed potatoes, to fetch me. Dennis had swallowed my story of the company financing my driving lessons and allowing me time off work to take driving lessons hook, line and sinker. He'd been impressed in fact and I felt ever so slightly guilty. By six o'clock the table was laden with egg and cress sandwiches, sausages on cocktail sticks, and crisps, and all the usual stuff. The doorbell rang - a formality because the front door was on the latch and the family arrived, all hugs kisses and banal chatter. I had turned down a hen night for this. I felt the tears trickling down my cheeks.

Nita embraced me, whispering, 'Come on Lynda, pull yourself together, this is your party, to show you how proud we are of you.'

'I know, Nita, and I'm okay really, it's just well, it's just the change I think, making me so stupid. I've got an appointment with Doctor Snelgrove next week.'

'Good,' she replied, 'because you've got your trip to Japan and the documentary coming up, you've got to be at your peak for both of those.' Dennis and the boys were getting louder now, the Subbuteo had been retrieved from the spare bedroom and a noisy game was in progress.

'You're not to put that back in the spare bedroom Dennis, now it's cleared you can make it into a nursery for Nita and Gary's baby.'

'Goal,' shouted Gary Lineker, aka Dennis. 'If it's a boy he'll be playing with us before you know it, just think - three generations of football stars in one house.' I looked at Nita, shaking my head. She whispered again, 'I've had another scan, Lynda, it's a girl, but we won't tell them yet, not until they get to the painting stage.'

'A girl, oh how wonderful,' I exclaimed, and reached for my hanky.

THIRTY

Aries: Understanding yourself and your needs is what it is all about this week. Your true feelings will surface and here lies what you really need from life.

The church bells from St Pancreas-in-the Meadow, a stone's throw away from our house, reached a crescendo and I lay rigid struggling to force my eyelids apart. My jaw dropped and I exerted upward pressure on my eyebrows with my thumbs but they remained stubbornly shut. My head belonged in hell, and I wished the rest of my body could follow it there, without further delay. As the sun streamed through the unlined flowery curtains, circa 1965, I screwed my eyelids tight and blinked quickly allowing my eyes to open - albeit narrow slits. The dressing table mirror revealed the new me, for I had apparently turned into a cabbage patch doll overnight. Swivelling my eyes right, a risky process, I found that Dennis had already apparently got up. That's if he had shared my bed with me last night. Intermittently thought waves limped through my exhausted brain, indistinct and muddled. I don't remember him coming to bed, but after a moment's hesitation I realized that I had no recollection of me going to bed either. I risked a glance under the coordinating brown and orange hydrangea covered sheet, lifting the cover with   the exhausted jelly like tentacles protruding from my shoulders -   a painful procedure. Waves of reminiscences circled my tired

189

brain, hitting the edges like a pin ball machine - grating and erratic. Yes, it was coming back to me now; the Kimono I was wearing wasn't a total surprise.

'Good Morning,' announced Dennis, with a bigger grin than Wallace of Wallace and Gromit fame, as he appeared with a loaded tray, wafting the aroma of filter coffee and freshly buttered toast around the bedroom. That was a first, and truly alarming.

'Oh my god, what did I do last night?' I asked. At least that what I thought I was saying but clearly Dennis was having some trouble understanding me. He raised an eyebrow and sniggered.

'Oh, talking Japanese are we now?' he continued, words and laughter tumbling out side by side. 'I have never seen you l-l-legless before, what an eye opener, Lynda; it was b-b-b-b-brill.' As my bottom lip drooped, he popped in a triangle of toast. I heaved.

'Oops,' he said, retrieving the marmalade laden parcel. 'Hell Lynda, you're going to have one hell of a hangover, but it was the best night ever. I saw a side to you last night that I've never seen in all our years together. You are absolutely b-b-bloody f-f-f-fantastic.' After a sip of coffee which unusually seemed to settle my stomach, I tried to sit up.

'I'll plump your pillows, shall I?' asked Wallace.

'OK,' I agreed. My poor addled brain was desperately searching for clues as to how I had achieved Dennis's accolade, the effects of which had even overflowed into the following morning. Normally, overindulgence, by me especially, would send him into a morose bundle of nerves, worrying about what his mother would say. His Mother, oh no, what had she

190

seen last night to hold against me for ever? And why wasn't she here now, victorious - berating me, preening herself?

'How is Ivy this morning?' My heart pounded involuntarily anticipating his grin becoming a defiant glare.

'She's fine as far as I know; she had an early night fortunately. I gave her the cocoa you left out early on, and to be honest I dropped in a couple of Mogodon just to settle her down as things were getting lively. The funny thing was Lynda, that when Cilla and all those girls appeared, Nita thought the same thing and she added a couple too, so she's still sleeping like a log I should think.'

'Have you checked on her this morning?' I squealed. Could she survive six Mogodon? Had we killed her? Who would be responsible for her death? Can three people be accused simultaneously of manslaughter, each unaware of the others actions. Would I be blameless as I was the first to overdose her?

Dennis, go and see if she's alright.' I ordered.

'Ok,' he agreed amicably, shifting his shoulders, but remaining immobile.

'Dennis,' I was verging on the hysterical now, 'go and see if she's alright.'

'Right, I will.' He retreated out the door hands waving wildly acknowledging defeat.

'What did he mean, when Cilla and the girls appeared?' I asked addressing the table lamp. Dennis loped back in, settling on the corner of the bed.

'She's fine, snoring like a bulldog.'

'She's definitely alive then?'

'Of course, she's alive; it'd take more than a couple of sleeping tablets to bump her off.' A couple or six I thought, but convinced now we wouldn't have to plan a funeral, I decided to change the subject. A lesson learnt - always discuss and agree your overdose arrangements with close family.

'So um, what was so good about last night then?'

'You really don't remember, do you?'

'No Dennis, I really don't remember.'

'Tee hee.'

'Tee bloody hee, Dennis just tell me, will you?'

'Well, let me see - do you want to know from the bit when you tried pole dancing on the squeegee mop, or from when your office girls did their Kylie Minogue dance routines for the lads from the carpentry shop?' My rapidly blinking eyes may have given me away, but I tried hard to nonchalantly ask, 'Oh, the lads, what time did they turn up then?' I queried, playing for time to search the memory banks, whilst my heart thudded and my jelly legs shook uncontrollably.

'Didn't look at my watch Lynda, too busy looking at you, you little sex bomb. Then the noise got so loud all the neighbours came round. I tell you what Lynda; I'm a bloody hero now. They are just so jealous that I've got a wife like you.' His chest expanded and pride burst out. He had never been proud of me before, well not that he had told me anyway.

'I told them, yes, she's a right little goer, why do you think I don't do overtime? Cos I'm knackered all the time that's why. I tell you Lynda, they're greener than Birds Eye Spinach with envy.' The thought of Spinach is not appealing on a dodgy stomach and I tried to visualize sandy beaches and shimmering pools. It didn't help. Dennis twitched.

'Do you need a bucket?'

'Don't change the subject Wallace - was I decent all the time? Please tell me I didn't strip or anything.'

'Oh no, I drew the line at that Lynda. You wanted to show them your tattoo, but I got to you before you unhooked your bra.'

'Tattoo?' I howled 'But I haven't got a tattoo, have I?' I quickly pulled my kimono apart, looking down rather too quickly and the room gently circled around me. Birds were twittering outside, or it may have been the oh so deaf one snoring.

'No, you haven't,' confirmed Dennis closely examining my chest. 'But I never know what you're getting up to nowadays, so I thought I'd best check.

'Do you know?' explained Dennis, 'for a while there Lynda, I was worried that you weren't the woman I married, well the girl really. But I can see now that I've got a cracking deal and it's me who's got some catching up to do.' Whispering now he added 'I think I was turning into a boring old fart you know.' He sounded surprised, but I was still dumbfounded that I had apparently turned from dredge to sex siren in one easy movement. Tunnel vision maybe? He'd called me a sex bomb. Wow they say life begins and all that, a couple of years late maybe but watch out world, here we come, together.

'I must say our Gary and Mark weren't best pleased though?'

'They didn't see me do anything, um, unsuitable did they?'

193

'No, not really,' said Dennis munching on my toast.

'Mark was busy kick boxing in the garden with Polly. She's got legs like a giraffe hasn't she? And Gary and Nita were having a bit of a barney about that girl with air bags for boobs — Mandy isn't it?'

'Oh dear, Mandy wasn't causing trouble between them was she?'

'Only in that she was promising to show us all, well I don't know quite what, but it was something to do with a cucumber anyhow. Anyway, Nita tried to get Gary to go home, but he wasn't keen to leave.'

'But Mandy stopped didn't she, tell me she stopped whatever she was doing.'

'Yes, cos you came in on the squeegee mop, minus your skirt that time.'

'Oh my god, how can I face everyone?'

'Fully clothed, hopefully. But it was a brilliant night, shame you can't remember it. Your new bra's definitely give you a bit of thrust,' he licked his lips almost drooling; 'your boobs look twice as big now.'

'I think it's coming back to me slowly, oh hello Nita.'

'Hello Granny to be, how are you feeling this morning? Not that I need to ask really,' she added. She plonked herself down beside me on the bed, causing shock waves and the inevitable happened. I was sick. Then she was sick. And Dennis, not quite the new man, left the room. We parcelled up the quilt and dropped it through the window to the yard below.

'We stayed the night, in the new nursery,' Nita explained, 'Gary had rather a lot to drink. Though not as much as you,' she looked at me accusingly. 'Lynda, there's something I've got to tell you.'

'If it's a complaint Nita I'm not ready to hear it yet, I'm feeling very fragile and rather foolish if you really want to know.'

'No, it's not about that, well not really, it's about the nursery in a way.'

'It's your choice Nita,' I interrupted, 'decorate it just how you want - any colour you like. I just want my granddaughter to have a little corner here, you know that. I can't believe I'll going to be a granny. Nita shrugged impatiently.

'I'll be right back.'

Maybe joining the granny brigade isn't going to be that easy I sighed and the baby wasn't even born yet. Perhaps her hormones are playing up. She's not usually like this, mysterious and broody. She reappeared with a boots bag and thrust it at me.

'Here,' she said, 'I've been meaning to give it to you for weeks but I kept hoping.......' she tailed off as I investigated the contents.

'A pregnancy testing kit? What's all this about. You know you're pregnant.' With a murmur of a smile on her face and a tremor in her voice she continued 'Yes, I do know I'm pregnant but I'm pretty sure you are too.' I felt the box crush between my fingers and looked down on my white knuckles. The sickness, the weight gain, the moods.......

'Go and do it now, while I'm here,' continued the soft voice. Her face was blurred though my tears. I felt her arms round me steering me to the bathroom. She hadn't moved when I returned, the little blue wand clenched tightly between my thumb and forefinger. I let out a sob, and she scooped me up from the floor where I had fallen. Cupping my head between her hands, she forced me to look at her, really look at her, gaze deep into her eyes through my tears.

'No more drinking for a while now,' she whispered.

'No more anything for the next twenty years.' I wailed.

'I'll go and get Dennis,' was all she could say.

Printed in Great Britain
by Amazon